Dougal's Diary

Sarah Stephenson

CROOKED
CAT

Dougal's Diary: 978-1-911381-27-3

First Green Line Edition, Crooked Cat Publishing, 2016

Discover us online:
www.crookedcatbooks.com

Join us on facebook:
www.facebook.com/crookedcatbooks

*Tweet a photo of yourself holding
this book to @crookedcatbooks
and something nice will happen.*

To my family & friends,
without whom I'd be lost.

Acknowledgements

First, my thanks go to Elaine Everest at The Write Place, without whose support, criticism and encouragement *Dougal's Diary* would have stayed in a drawer. To Natalie, for her patience in helping a dinosaur join Facebook, Twitter and the modern world. And to the rest of the class, who listened to the various stages of Dougal's development and actually found it fun.

To my father Tom, my brother Michael and daughter Hannah, for always believing in and encouraging my writing.

A very special thanks to Hilary Johnson for her valuable advice.

Then, of course there's Dougal, without whom there would be no tale to tell.

And lastly but never least, an enormous thank you to Laurence and Stephanie Patterson at Crooked Cat Publishing, for believing Dougal's story had legs. I received news of their interest in the book whilst cooking for a large summer party. In my excitement, I screamed so loudly a guest dashed into the kitchen, fearing I'd burnt myself.

Sarah Stephenson
November 2016

The Author

Sarah, who grew up in Bristol, now lives in South-East London with two dogs, the occasional grandchild and a lot of mess. She's had a chequered career as ballet dancer, cook, cleaning lady, salesgirl of outsize underwear in Littlewoods and actor. As an actor she worked mainly in the theatre: plays ranging from Shakespeare to improvised, both comedy and tragedy.

Cooking combines two of her passions: travel and people. She's catered in barges in Burgundy, private houses in America, many stately homes in England, run a delicatessen, a stall at a farmers' market and been a judge on the Great Taste Food Awards. Good opportunities for hearing about the lives of others.

Her need to write began with letters, sending home news of her adventures. At seventeen, travelling alone on the Trans-Siberian Railway and across the Sea of Japan. In Greece, as a drama student, when their van blew up at the Springs of Daphne and they explored the mainland, riding on bread vans and tractors before selling their blood for a fiver and hitch-hiking home on a lorry. Or in Morocco on a solo trip, in pre-mobile phone days, when she was chucked off a bus in the desert and found herself surrounded by hundreds of camels and similar numbers of men, all in local dress.

Since then Sarah hasn't stopped scribbling and joining The Write Place, a writing class in Dartford, encouraged her to put the contents of numerous exercise books into something more concrete.

These days Sarah chooses less adventurous holidays, but might well send one of her characters off on a trek she doesn't feel brave enough to make.

Dougal's Diary is Sarah's first book.

Dougal's Diary

The Introduction

As Uncle John, who later became one of my favourite friends, says, 'It's the very doggyness of the dog that makes us recognisable. No other species is as diverse, whether in height, shape, colour, hair or temperament.'

I'm Dougal, a labradoodle, the designer dog first created in Australia to be the ultimate canine companion and guide dog for human beings with sight impairment or total blindness. Dogs who have no odour, even in wet weather, low shedding for those with allergies, active during the day, ready to cuddle up on the sofa with a novel at night.

Who on earth wrote this drivel? I stink when wet, am a lap dog through and through, whatever time of day, and to my knowledge have never read a novel. We're costly hybrids, not as expensive as a Prius but requiring more fuel; a crossbreed and model of a modern dog, if not everyone's cup of tea. Yet some folk are so desperate for us puppies there are countries selling ferrets as labradoodles, proving that we're popular, there's a killing to be made and people are mad.

Labradoodle – half Labrador, half poodle, the perfect mix, but which half?

Personality of a Poodle
Looks like a sissy dog but is not
Needs long walks to keep calm and fit
May suffer separation anxiety

Personality of a Labrador
Loves kids

Tummy on legs (food obsessed)
Man's best friend

Personality of a Labradoodle
Can't be put in a crate unless very young
Might share the stomach of a Labrador
Problems with jumping up

We love people, tend to be meet and greet creatures and are all bonkers. Like jumpers, we come in a variety of colours and sizes. Supposedly, we have the laid-back qualities of a Labrador, the brains of a poodle and don't moult. As for me, I have the legs, chest and hair of a poodle, the head, nose and stomach of a Labrador, and am fitted with the simplest plumbing system.

For those unfamiliar with the internal workings of a Labrador, the gut is a vast tube, along which food and other objects travel in either direction. Duration: anything from two minutes to ten days. Should I have colonic irrigation, I'd be able to see last week's intake: dog biscuits, rubber duck, sausage, a football (outer covering only) and one sock. I have a penchant for socks. Would have included child's plastic telephone but at the eleventh hour it was removed by strong saline solution.

If anyone doubts a Lab's gluttony, Mandy from No 19 ate a whole casserole while it was bubbling on the stove. How she'd shifted her huge frame on to the cooker was what amazed her family most. Once kilos of cabbage were added to her diet, her weight and appetite dropped with the wind. And Bessie from the village was so consumed by greed she ate four frozen rib-eye steaks and two lamb kebabs. The sticks came out the bottom end, whole, minus the meat.

Obviously, food dominates most of my waking hours but, as the books tell you, you can either have a fat hungry dog or a thin hungry dog. And I am a very thin, very hungry dog, not at all what I planned.

I would like to think I've the brains of a poodle, but that's highly debatable.

My Diary 2012-2013

The first few weeks were added later when I had a better grasp of English.

The Union of Magnificent Millie and Barney Riddle

I'm the product of an arranged marriage, my history a DH Lawrence, *Lady Chatterley* kind of tale. Mother, an aristocratic beauty; Father, the canine version of a plumber – an odd choice one might think. Her family tree was indeed impressive, finer than royalty and cor, what a looker! She won every beauty pageant going and the dogs in the park swooned at the sight of her, or so the story goes. However, she was built like a racehorse. Not many go shopping for a puppy and return with a foal, do they? Hence a small stud was sought.

A few enthusiastic suitors, Apple Jack, Perfect Pete and Yogi Bear, attempted the deed, but bottled out when faced with the Magnificent Millie, leaving Barney Riddle from Essex to sire the eleven of us.

6ᵗʰ January 2012. Margate, Kent

After nine weeks, our delivery took place in a large rambling house at the edge of the sea. I began quite small, could sit on one hand like a bag of sweets or five butcher's sausages, had a long body, short legs similar to a blond rat, only cuter. Big brown eyes, hair that might grow, might curl or just might not. And as to my size, would I turn into a giant? Somewhere in my forebears lurked a miniature poodle. Would he have any bearing on my height? I'd arrived minus a pedigree and with no guarantee.

We had a blissful childhood romping around the house,

sleeping on sofas and watching Sky TV News, History and Animal channels – spoilt, I guess. And although we had no desire to flee the nest and venture into a strange new land where all fun is banned and the words 'No' and 'Bad Dog' would become all too familiar, we were under no illusion: Margate was temporary. Our futures lay elsewhere.

As the time to leave crept ever closer, the classes kicked off: pee on paper, sit on command and lastly, the most vital lesson of all, find the right owner. Never fall into the wrong hands. Puppies, you have a choice. Use it.

9ᵗʰ March
The adverts went out.

Eleven Adorable Labradoodle Puppies For Sale.

For two entire days the phone lines were jammed. Then the browsers arrived. They came, looked, left and revisited. Some bought, others borrowed and returned – not hypoallergenic enough.

Does a man choose a dog that looks like him or grow to resemble his dog? How much of the man is in the dog or indeed the dog in the man? I knew I must not doze off when being viewed, so hid.

I was the last of the litter to choose my boss. No one had taken my fancy until a woman turned up, depressed from Battersea, a dumping ground for dogs filled with Staffordshire bull terriers, desperate for the love they were unlikely to find. None could be rehomed with children under eighteen.

The woman arrived with a child, a badly behaved boy who wasn't told off, or not much. They ran along the beach together and chased each other round the house. Then he sat on her lap, demanding Ribena and crisps. Now this looked promising. I crawled out from under the sofa. And it got better. She spoke of walled gardens, woods and streams. Mentioned food: cooking for banquets in stately homes. Naturally my stomach played a part in my choice, but not entirely, for I saw in her the qualities I yearned for: freedom of spirit with a dash of domestication. I could retain my independence and live like a king, if only I was owned by her.

When they left, unable to make a decision, I was inconsolable. She was after a smaller dog. What if I promised not to grow?

Then a call came from a lay-by. I was wanted after all, but could I wait two weeks while she went to India? Little did I know this trip would dominate my diet for ever. Chicken Vindaloo? No way! I'm talking rice, the staple diet of Indians and me.

25th March

Two days to go. Three of us still in Kent. Prue, me with no name and Winston. Prue staying put, Winston waiting for his owners to return from California, me scanning the skies for an Air India plane from Delhi.

When we leave our mother, we are babies still, our personalities in embryo state, only beginning the journey to who we'll eventually become. Uncertain what lies ahead, we have to learn how to read the human mind, get the hang of toilet training and discover, however cute a puppy you are, some people hate dogs and that's just the way it is.

Homesick, I hadn't even left. I couldn't sleep, couldn't eat. So young, yet wasting away. I sat by the door, not exactly a sad evacuee with suitcase and label, rather a wistful puppy with favourite toy and blanket, belongings linking my old life to the new.

27th March

Had I chosen well and landed on my paws? My heart was in my mouth, the contents of my stomach in the car, as I vomited my way to London, the entire seventy miles. When I entered my new home in Greenwich, I was devastated. From tearful farewells I'd come to this. Was it a prison or Battersea Dogs' Home? There were gates everywhere and a crate large enough to house a lion. Barely twelve weeks old and I could smell a rat.

There is no one quite so scary as a women in the wrong who is convinced she's right or anything so determined as a labradoodle puppy born in Kent. Start as you mean to go on, they tell you. I did. She didn't. I howled louder than the beasts of the Serengeti plains, then climbed on top of the cage and refused to budge. She threw down a blanket, then disappeared upstairs, closing the gate behind her. That was it. I jumped from crate to stairs, five kilos of supernatural strength charging at the bars till I broke through, carrying the stair gate on my back. The siege ended with one dazed puppy, one bedraggled owner and a skip full of steel. My final thought before passing out was, had I made the right choice?

There was no going back!

28th March

'Jane, dear, if this is your new baby, he's going to be a monster.' I woke to find someone stroking my ears. It wasn't my new boss. 'Whatever was going on last night? I thought I was living next to a zoo, that or a slaughter house. Had no idea which of the emergency services to call.' She took a deep breath then rattled on. 'I was having my nightcap. Before I'd come to a decision, I must have drifted off.'

'I was attempting to put him to bed, Mrs King.'

'Not in that.' The old woman looked frighteningly like a racoon and smelt of peppermint.

'I thought he'd love it.'

'Well, I wouldn't want to go in there, dear. I'm in a rush now, but I'll pop back later with a bottle. We can enjoy a drink and wet the baby's head.'

'Rather a waste of good gin.'

'It is a special day, dear. And I'll bring a pile of newspapers. Those training pads are a frightful expense. By the way, Jane, I'm thrilled you got a boy. I so love men.' Then, waggling her finger at me, she said, 'Don't you dare misbehave.' And with those stern words, she let herself out.

New Boss told me not to worry, her bark was worse than her bite.

10 a.m.

Watch out, world, here I come. Spruced up with red collar and lead, I bounced into the park with the energy of an Olympic athlete. I couldn't remember my name, was only vaguely aware to whom I belonged and when faced with masses of legs all wearing jeans, not a clue. My boss lost control of my lead as I chased every bike, scooter and pushchair, then flew through the gates after the wrong pair of legs. Near collision with a juggernaut – saved by a lollipop lady. Once safely back inside the park, three boxers dived straight for the jugular.

'They are only showing off,' said their owner. 'It's a pecking order kind of thing.' Really! It took four men to pull them off. Was this some strange initiation ceremony? I'd almost gone home in a box. Told I was very brave.

Back home, I aimed for the paper and missed, but somehow managed to pee through the gaps. Urine drip, drip, dripping through the floorboards; the smell would last for days. The Boss proved very understanding and said she was glad I wasn't a cat. Strange since she bought a dog, but I, too, am glad I am not a cat. By the time Mrs King stumbled in with gin and newspapers, I was safely tucked up in bed.

'Here are the papers I promised.' I ran to greet her.

'That's an awful lot of *Mails*, Mrs King.'

How much urine were they expecting me to produce?

'You have to be so careful with the press these days, Jane. I know I'm in safe hands with Mr Murdoch. It's by Royal Appointment.'

I was impressed. The Boss looked doubtful.

'Jane, dear, it's obvious the Queen uses it for her puppies.' Mrs King's eyes flashed in the light. 'That is why the weekend *Mail* has so many pages. He can think of it as royal toilet paper.' Clearly, the human mind was completely incomprehensible.

'Now, let's get things straight, Jane. I can't do walkies, but I can babysit if you're out late,' Out! I'd never been alone in my life. Would she let me sit on her lap? 'I don't want paying, leave me a drop of gin and we'll call it quits. Besides, he'll be company, except when the privet's flowering.' The Boss looked bemused, to say the least.

'Your hedge, dear. Gives me asthma.' What was this place? As my eyelids drooped, the last sounds I heard were of drinks being poured. I never knew if I'd been anointed or not.

29th March

Off we went by car. Had no idea traffic-watching could be such fun. Leapt into the park with no less enthusiasm than yesterday, only to be attacked by a fox terrier who hated puppies. Took me thirty minutes to stop crying. No one told me I was brave.

Just when the confidence of youth was disappearing faster than a ferret down a rabbit hole, I received torrents of abuse from an elderly gent who said I should be wearing a muzzle, reported to the police and put down. His grandson was playing cricket. I only chased his ball. Shall I survive this life? Will I see six months? Oh, to be back in Margate.

Seven p.m. brought my first pub visit; the welcome was massive, experience brief. Became overexcited, peed on the floor, barked at a bulldog, sent home. From entrance to exit: a mere eight minutes. Before bed we walked round the block in the dark. All wildlife had run away. I would have, too, had I not been on the lead, except I'd have dashed across the traffic, meaning I have less intelligence than a fox. Must point out: foxes are used to traffic, I am not.

2nd April. Blackheath Veterinary Surgery

We were up with the larks. Not being an early bird, I confess to struggling. We had an urgent meeting with Alan, the man overseeing my physical well-being, who costs a bomb. So although our rapport was instantaneous, it's vital we rarely meet.

After my check-up, that seems unlikely. I have one testicle missing (unaware I had any), am underweight and the final blow: I have nothing between my ears. All grey matter is packed inside a pea that rolls around this copious space. If my boss left with post-traumatic stress disorder, I forgot all about it in two seconds flat, proving Alan 100% right.

Later, we came across a bunch of old Labs discussing their health: cancer, strokes, hip-replacements. They're on chemo and strong medication. I've taken an oath never to grow old.

3rd April

I am collecting friends fast – both canine and human varieties: Titch and Tiger, owners Carol and Andy. Titch is a large Yorkshire terrier, called Titch because he was expected to be tiny. By the time he'd grown past his name, it was too late; the name had stuck. Titch hates all large dogs except me. He's clueless I'll be one soon.

Tiger is a massive Dogue de Bordeaux / bull mastiff-cross. Forty-eight kilos of pure muscle and growing fast. We play-box for hours, just like big cats – possibly the reason for his name: that and his stripes. Despite his size, he's terrified of everything: noise, terriers, water – anything larger than a puddle.

If it's true that squeezed inside all small dogs is a monster hound desperate to escape, and inside all large dogs lies a tiny puppy longing for a lap, I worry what I'll find hidden in me.

4th April **

This is an important diary entry so I've put two stars beside it, to ensure its position of value. His name I've written in bold.

Today, I played with an attractive dog called **Chester.** **Chester** is a Staffie-cross from Battersea who looks like a small version of Tiger. He's extremely popular and I want to be his friend. Here ends the important bit. What happened next can go to the shredder.

12 p.m.
The child is here. It has been a black hour. He chucked me out of the room and slammed the door. If I'd come from Battersea I'd have killed him. There have been moments when I wish I had.

2 p.m.
We're both on the sofa, learning to be friends. Thanks to *CBeebies*, I am able to recognise all the animals in Noah's Ark. This will help if I meet any hippos in Greenwich.

The boy has a name: Jacob. Jacob's teeth are falling out, a problem we share, and he had my fullest support until I found he has a tooth fairy that brings him money. Should he use the money to buy treats and give me half, I would consider that fair and like him more. Sharing is what pals do. Or we could do swaps: sweets for dog biscuits.

9ᵗʰ April
We have a small terrorist in the park. Titch has lost his ability to distinguish small dogs from large and is savaging all he meets. Poor Carol can no longer chat to her friends: the only words she utters are variations on the theme of 'sorry'.

13ᵗʰ April
Best morning yet: ate fox poo, scared a child, nicked a football, chased a bike, then slept.

Come late afternoon, we went to town to meet The Boss's sister, Hannah, and boyfriend, Luke. My first train ride to the great metropolis. So many rules, so much to learn. Mustn't sit on seats, sniff bottoms or stick my nose in people's shopping. And rush hour is daunting; traffic crawling along roads like armies of ants. Needed carrying across the Strand.

Hannah and Luke had bagged a table outside the *Koha Restaurant* in St Martin's Court. While they chatted, the waiter gave me water and titbits, took my photo and sent it to his wife in Slovakia. Crowds clustered round me like wasps over jam. By the time they'd finished their meal, Hannah, Luke, the waiter, his wife, their friends in Slovakia and all the customers sitting outside the *Koha Restaurant* had decided I was so cute they couldn't live without a labradoodle puppy.

I pranced cockily back to the station past men hanging out of pubs, smoking and queuing up to pet me. A cracking night out! My only blip was crapping on Platform 3 at Charing Cross. If the story leaks, will the waiter, Hannah, Luke and all the villagers in Slovakia still want a puppy like me?

Am now dragging her into every pub we pass. The Boss is complaining people will consider her an alcoholic.

14th April

'Sorry, contrite, apologetic.' Despite help from the thesaurus, Carol is running out of words as Titch's behaviour continues to spiral. She contemplated branching out into other languages but, being no linguist and fearing the owners of the dogs Titch had savaged might think she was taking the piss and lynch her, called an animal psychologist instead. I'm watching this space. If large dogs behaved like this they'd be put down.

15th April

My life is plummeting fast. I lifted my leg to pee and fell over. Sure hope no one was watching or, worse still, videoing the moment. Next, I jumped up at a lady smoking a fag. Didn't mean to, promise, I mistook it for a treat. Oh dear! Whichever way one looks at it, I've blown it. I'm off to puppy classes. Training was not on my agenda or part of the package I originally signed up for.

Attempts to cock my leg are greeted with mirth. Why am I doing this when squatting is so much simpler?

16ᵗʰ April

Down in the dumps! Conned rotten. Only booked in with Simon, a well-known Greenwich dog walker. Barely here a month and I'm to be booted out for six whole days while The Boss works. What happened to those stately home banquets I spent weeks salivating over? Will someone please save me from this diet of tasteless biscuit? If The Boss cooked for a dog food company, I could eat fish and chips, smoked salmon, even pukka pie biscuits. Now, that would be something.

Meanwhile, I remain in the dumps.

20ᵗʰ April

I'm saved! Simon has no space on his books. The Boss will be forced to rethink and have me with her in the kitchen. I could be her personal taster and wash up – wouldn't want paying.

Out of luck; I'm off to Simon's dog-walking friend, a Slavic princess named Miriam. Rubbing shoulders with royalty sounds good. Mrs King would approve. I'm having day care only, returning each night in case I forget who owns me.

Staying in a palace! I'll need to adopt some airs and graces.

22ⁿᵈ April

Not a good Titch day: he tried savaging three large dogs in one fell swoop. Luckily for them, his mouth is small. Not being a rescue dog, there is no excuse for his behaviour.

25ᵗʰ April

After three days with Miriam, her daughters and dog Biba, whom I worship, I would prefer to board. Tip-top food: freshly made sheep's curd, lentil soup and bones to chew between meals which might not be on the menu at Bojnice Castle. When it was time to go I hung back, disinclined to leave.

'You've got to go home to your mummy,' the girls told

me.

Mummy, no way! That's when I knew I had to give The Boss a name and it sure wouldn't be *Mummy*.

My only disappointment was her home. It was neither castle, nor palace: just an ordinary house. Not stately at all. My biggest surprise was coming face to face with the suppliers of the curds cheese – a flock of sheep in her small back garden. Amiable enough creatures, but relieved they didn't tag along on our Greenwich Park walks.

2nd May

There's no need for police protection in our road. As a first-rate busybody, Mrs King does a better job. She has a hotline direct to the police, maybe an undercover agent, no one is entirely sure, but behind all twitching curtains is the vague outline of old King's nose pressed against the windowpane. That lady is the human equivalent of a sniffer dog.

8th May

I've zero enthusiasm for balls, but have developed a deep interest in my dental hygiene and am chewing sticks like they're going out of fashion.

Thought I'd got the hang of toilet training, but the paper keeps moving. It's now in the garden with the back door open. Busting a gut after a long walk, I rushed in desperate for the paper. Wrong move! If I'm not meant to use it, why is it there? These rules are beyond me.

Tomorrow, I'm off to town again, my second trip to the big smoke, this time to meet Uncle John, a man famed for his firework displays.

9th May

The day began with a fabulously wet walk in the woods, one I made full use of, especially the mud. My hair colour changed from cream to black, my scent from the acceptable to nose-holding bad.

After a quick shower with washing-up liquid, no proper rinsing, suds clearly visible but smelling pleasantly of Fairy

Liquid Original, I was considered fit to travel.

In Bloomsbury, Uncle John was waiting – no sign of fireworks, but with treats I couldn't enjoy with my usual gusto as starting to feel crook. I vomited all over his carpet and throughout their entire lunch, a light froth similar to whipped egg whites. Uncle John said not to worry: being the same colour as the carpet, it wouldn't show.

The Boss took full responsibility. If only she'd rinsed me properly. By licking my coat, I'd imbibed litres of undiluted soap my stomach was unable to contain. The bubbles had to go somewhere and out they kept coming.

Uncle John considered her argument scientifically unsound and when she picked up the phone to call *Proctor & Gamble (UK)*, suggested it might be a waste of everyone's time.

We left for me to cough and puke all the way home, right through the night and into the park. The moment I heard the words 'kennel cough', I knew I was a goner.

Off to see Alan. I'm so highly contagious we had to go after surgery hours. I took one look at my vet and thought he'd turned to bee-keeping. He wore plastic gloves, a mask and carried a spray can to disinfect all the surfaces I touched.

The verdict was both good and bad. I'll begin with the bad: I've lost four kilos. The good: my lost testicle has been found – whoopee! And, I have trauma of the larynx: my throat torn to shreds through excessive dental hygiene. The chewing of sticks was not a wise move; I should have flossed. I left with a precautionary dose of kennel cough vaccine.

To celebrate the arrival of testicle number two, I humped Chester. The additional testicle has given me feelings which exert the urge to do press-ups, only on Chester.

Chester lives with George, an old black Lab. They are owned by a man whose name we do not know. He has such long legs I have never seen his face, but he has to be kind. The dogs sleep in his bed. Night-time must be a tight squeeze. The man has a wife and two small children – that's a lot of legs. I hope the others' are shorter than his.

To sleep on a bed is my dearest wish. In a bed sounds too warm for a hound born wearing a woolly onesie – unless recently returned from a muddy walk.

13th May

The dreaded training starts tomorrow. I'm booked in to see Simone, a teacher who believes in praise and treats. If that sounds too good to be true, it is. We have to listen, learn and attend not one week but eight. On the other hand, I'm lucky to live now rather than the eighties when Barbara Woodhouse ruled the roost. Gone are the choke chains, corporal punishment and smacks with a rolled-up copy of the *Mail*. In come sausage treats, spray collars and gentle words.

And better still, when one has eaten the Christmas turkey, no longer is it OK to say, 'You stupid bastard, just wait till I get my hands on you.' Instead the language has changed to, 'Oh dear, bad decision, Dougal. Now, you silly dog, once you've finished our lunch, let's have a little quiet time and see if you can make good choices.'

Note the word *silly*. Under no circumstances must the word *stupid* be used – giving negative signals. After hearing this, I couldn't wait for my first class.

Simone and Simon! These names are most confusing. Lucky neither of them are dogs, or one shout and they'd both come running. It's like the banker who wanted to call his dogs Debit and Credit, until some dear friend explained that to a dog the names would sound exactly the same.

14th May

What a waste of time. Learnt to walk on a loose lead, sit, stay, leave and lastly enter the hall like the perfect *Crufts* dog: running beside its owner, eyes fixed on theirs. A bunch of stuff to take in, especially if you don't want to do it. I mucked around, refused to take the class seriously and was handed a yellow card – unfairly saddled with a bad reputation.

15th May

Today I forgot everything I'd learnt. Chased a squirrel across a road, looked dim when asked to sit, had excellent recall when offered treats, then buggered off to meet my mates. Despite the sensitive approach, training remains tricky; five steps forward, ten steps back.

I hope our bosses realise however perfectly trained their pet, there are times when it will revert to being a dog. Behaving badly is far more fun.

16th May

Stonkingly good day! Terrified an entire nursery school and left muddy paws on the most elegantly-suited woman in the park. Once home, I ate two brown socks, the tacks off the telephone wires, hacked through the skirting board, burst two footballs, was halfway through eating one of them and it wasn't even lunchtime.

By 5 p.m., I'd eaten my lead, dug three large holes in the garden, chased next door's cat and chewed the leg off a chair. I'd call that success.

17th May

After sleeping for fifteen hours I woke to find I'd grown. I'm now ten times the size of a pigeon, twice the size of dachshund and a quarter the way up the plum tree. Had to endure non-stop criticism; my behaviour yesterday wasn't up to much.

Paul popped round to mend telephone wires and fill holes in skirting board.

18th May

Stuff this well-behaved-dog lark. Have decided to be one hundred per cent perfect five per cent of the time. I was home alone and bored out of my brains when I discovered wallpaper interestingly tasty and easy to tear. Since time was on my side, I gnawed the putty out of the skirting boards and neatly removed the new tacks from the telephone wires. I thought of them as baby teeth, but somehow couldn't imagine a fairy coming.

The Boss is furious. I'm in the doghouse. Only Paul is happy: further work equals extra cash. Could we go into business?

19th May

Am I the fastest dog in the park or what? Only chased two whippets and overtook them, no problem. Has any labradoodle puppy ever beaten a whippet before? This had to be a Guinness Book moment. Boss said they weren't even running in second gear; in fact, they'd barely moved out of neutral.

She's such a spoilsport. I never get the chance to boast.

20th May

Finally, The Boss has been shamed. Nothing like the stocks, not a public humiliation, but you can see the guilt spilling from her guts. I am experiencing separation anxiety and that's why I'm destroying the house. Now I have this anxiety thing and can't be left, Mrs King is babysitting.

She arrived, hands full and breathless. In her desire to reduce the time spent communing with our hedge, Mrs King raced up the drive at such rocket speed, she brought about the very asthma attack she was trying to avoid. Honestly, I thought she was going to croak.

In pulling out her puffer, she dropped a bag of sweets and the *Daily Mail*, but somehow hung on to the gin. Once she got her breath back, her mouth opened and words streamed out. The Boss says she suffers from verbal diarrhoea.

'I'm here, dear, so you don't have to fret.' I wasn't, but put on a sad expression. 'Now, if it's all right with you, I'm going to watch my programme.'

Mrs King poured herself a drink and offered me a humbug. I didn't refuse. The taste of peppermint was odd, but pleasantly sweet. The rest of the evening was spent in front of the telly watching snooker and sucking toffees. I swallowed mine whole, hence my pleasure was briefer than hers. The *Daily Mail* was for her TV viewing; relieved, as

I'm now house-trained.

It'd be easy to nod off in front of the snooker, if you weren't watching it with Mrs King who is as mad on ball games as chatting. By the time The Boss turned up, I was so informed I could have won a sports quiz. Have decided, I'm a companion, not a dog.

Mrs King isn't part of the racoon family. She wears horn-rimmed glasses.

21st May

At 6 p.m., we drove to Charlton, another route under my belt. In class, we worked on jumping-up problems which Simone, our instructor, thinks I'll grow out of. So why, I'd like to ask, am I bothering? If we were tested on satnav skills, I'd be top of the class, top dog.

Eureka! I'd got it, my name for her – after all, she is my top dog. Bit of a mouthful so shall abbreviate it, and call her TD instead. Giving her a name has really cemented our relationship.

22nd May

School isn't for me; absolutely, positively, not my kind of thing. I'd happily skive off, truant, or better still get an ASBO. TD is determined none of the above will happen. We'll see.

23rd May

Will my education ever be over? This private tuition is torture for the soul. What if I self-harm or get an eating disorder?

24th May

The answer to yesterday's question is no.

28th May

Dammit! Back in class to find I've been rumbled. I'm not suffering from separation anxiety, merely behaving badly. I knew that, but how come Simone does? I'm now being left with a carrot, chews filled with peanut butter and the radio on.

Next week we are learning how to pass food on the pavement with a halo on our heads. I'm going to have a sickie. There's no way I'm attending that class.

10 p.m.

Thank you, *Radio 2*. It transpires the requirements for a healthy puppy are not only a phenomenal twenty hours of sleep but two to six thousand calories a day. I'm starting to panic. Will I reach adulthood? Might I get rickets? And how many calories does a carrot possess? I can't depend on TD.

Now I know Greenwich is a Royal Borough, I've become a hundred per cent Royalist.

29th May

Carol could pass for an escapologist. She's enveloped in leads: short leads, long leads, choke leads, retractable, metal, plastic, leather. And as for Titch, Titch is filled with liver treats. If he doesn't growl at a dog he gets a treat. His weight gain is proof of his improved behaviour.

30th May

Three strikes and you're out. I've had a warning. Behave or else!

Cousin Maggie is coming to lunch. After thirty-seven operations she is still walking. Her bravery puts me to shame. Maggie is so frail I must, absolutely not, jump up. Even putting my head on her lap could cause a collapse. Her stomach is now so small TD is preparing food that would sit well in a doll's house.

Maggie, who owns two elderly cats, loves dogs with a passion but, due to poor health, is nervous around large, boisterous puppies.

Since her lap was off-limits, how could I gain her trust? I wasn't prepared to spend the remainder of the day licking my privates in some impossible *Strictly Come Dancing* leg contortion in order to impress, but I did need something sensational, on a par with pulling a rabbit out of a hat. By the time the BBQ was lit I'd come up with a brilliant plan.

At 1 p.m., Maggie arrived with the lovely Lois, one of my treasured friends. Maggie looks like a Greek goddess with pale eyes and Lois – just a goddess. Truly, I believe Lois is the reincarnation of Florence Nightingale. Whenever TD is sick she's off shopping, driving and doing bits dogs can't yet do. Though I believe my brother Branston is being trained in these matters.

They sat on the patio, sipping wine and talking in hushed tones. Maggie can only speak in a whisper so the volume was kept low out of respect. Meanwhile, I was busy dismantling the dry stone wall that separates the flower beds from the paths, a task I believed showed strength, prowess and masculinity. Something no cat can do. I'd never seen a cat with a brick in its mouth.

If a job's worth doing, it's worth doing beautifully. I removed them quietly, in keeping with the day, and was about to stand back and admire my handiwork, two entire walls laid neatly across the lawn, when the heavens opened and the party rushed inside.

'Oh, Jane, no!' cried Lois. 'Our food!'

'Don't worry. I'll fetch the BBQ.'

'What, into the kitchen?' Alarm bells were ringing.

'Oh, it'll be fine,' said TD confidently. 'Remember the fun we had with the Mongolian cookpot?' Before her sentence could be fully digested, TD was struggling in with the barbie.

The kitchen took a week to clean, four days to dry out and three to paint. When my masterpiece was discovered two days later I received neither the praise I'd yearned for nor the complaints I probably deserved. In comparison to the damage done to the kitchen my garden makeover was trifling.

Branston's coming-out parade as a mobility dog happens next June. It's similar to the Trooping the Colour – minus the Queen and not on TV. I gather Mongolian cookpots are designed for indoor use.

31ˢᵗ May

Today a lot of humping went on. I humped Chester. George humped Chester. Me on top, George underneath. Chester is the prize in our DCG sandwich.

Tiger won't be in the park for a whole week. He is having the snip. The next time I see him, he'll be an it. The price of the op varies according to size. His testicles can't weigh much, so must be cheap. I'm keeping mine.

1ˢᵗ June

Maggie has rung to say her cats, Casper and Constanza, have finally learnt their names, definitely, 100% or almost. What! It's taken these cats of seventeen or eighteen – who knows what it is in cat years – plus an additional nine lives each, to reach a point when they just may recognise their names. When I think of all the thousands of years they've spent adapting to humans, I am staggered to find cats that stupid.

2ⁿᵈ June

I haven't the foggiest how the kangaroo got its hop, but I do know how the labradoodle got its jump. Jacob's been practising backflips and handstands in our hall. They're off to the circus to see clowns, horses and budgies – a farcical combination. Jacob says in years gone by circuses employed elephants, lions, monkeys and poodles – information I needed to know. It's blatantly obvious: my love of jumping, dancing and applause is in the blood!

Wearing fabulous costumes, they leapt through burning hoops, walked on tightropes on their back legs and boxed, the same way Tiger and I do, except we don't wear gloves. I might even be a descendant of famous poodles such as Cookie and Ruiliz. Oh, to perform in Paris for royalty!

I wish I was totally poodle, not this half-breed. Would I be more neurotic without my Labrador blood? Am I better off as I am? Who knows? Who cares? I love being me.

Now I know my history I can cock my leg without falling over.

3ʳᵈ June

Deeply worried about my sight; I'm getting square eyes. Forced to watch the Queen on a barge. Didn't find it personally inspiring; a few corgis would have added interest. Surprised Her Majesty didn't think of it. Possibly a health and safety issue or perhaps Prince Philip objected. Fairy cakes covered in fruit went some way to compensating. TD said they looked like Union Jacks. All I could see were blueberries and raspberries. TD kept her topping till last. I ate my cake whole.

Simon had nineteen dogs to walk today, nine sleeping over – on his bed! I hope TD hears this and takes note.

4ᵗʰ June

A week's grace; thanks to the bank holiday, my class isn't running.

5ᵗʰ June

Great news! Titch is on a diet and off the lead. Carol is back talking to her friends. This is one happy story.

6ᵗʰ June

Teeth giving me gyp. Chewing all I can find: socks, teddies, trainers – anything that hasn't been specifically designed for dogs.

Mrs King is off to dentist. Like mine, her teeth are problematic. At least hers aren't falling out all over the carpet. She should go to *Pets at Home*. Those rawhide chews would help her. Humans do chew bones; they call it *corn on the cob*.

TD continues to moan. My obsession with Chester is ruining our walks. Is it my fault I've got feelings?

Chasing squirrels is challenging.

10ᵗʰ June

When Mrs King told me the menu I gratefully accepted her luncheon invitation. She does a nice ham and cheese pie and I love crumble and custard.

4 p.m.

We've been glued to repeats of the *Great British Bake Off* all afternoon. Mrs King's been having a right old go at the telly, considers Mary Berry hopeless. If she overheard her, Mary Berry wouldn't be gutted. Mrs King is unintelligible. She has removed her teeth. They're sitting in a glass of water, staring at me. Remembering TD's words, *'her bark is worse than her bite'*, I worry will the teeth stay in the glass?

Mrs King says Paul Hollywood can't put a foot wrong. Is she biased? Privately, I believe Mrs King is seething. She applied to be a contestant on the show, fell at the first fence, didn't even reach the prelims and is blaming Mary Berry.

I now know I'm a dog and a companion.

11ᵗʰ June

I usually run a mile when I hear the old Labs droning on about their ailments, but today's topic was food. Right up my street, or so I thought, except they can't eat this, can't eat that. Lack of teeth, I imagined. Nope, allergies. And they must have five a day, of what I've no idea. Discovered all dogs are lactose intolerant. How depressing; I love cheese.

Dragged into class. What a nightmare. The others must have spent the last fortnight practising – oh goody, goody them! As expected, I left without the halo, more like a crown of thorns. If I don't buck my ideas up, I won't graduate and will be forced to retake the whole course. Bollocks!

12ᵗʰ June

Fantastic news! I've got a job! TD's had a run of evening work, hence hours spent with Mrs King. On top of that there's been a spate of burglaries, so the old girl, who's put the entire neighbourhood on red terror alert, is policing the area with me, her unofficial police puppy. I need a bullet-proof vest. I'm too young to die.

14ᵗʰ June

When I hear his name it's his scent I first recall. Rich,

seductive: sweeter than a tin of tuna and better far than sausages or bacon butties. My nostrils quiver, excitement pounds through my capillaries and I'm fully fired. Oh, Chester.

18ᵗʰ June

The news flew round the park like wildfire. Our famous dog-walker, Simon, is in hospital. The dogs he walks are in bits. As per usual, humans missed the point. What we dogs should do is follow our masters to the hospital, either on foot or, better still, travel in the ambulance with them.

You'd think a private hospital would be thrilled to let Simon have his dogs help him through, not the actual operation – our hygiene scarcely being up to scratch – but as visitors, or overnight. Here we are blessed with special powers to aid recovery, being trained as PAT (Pets As Therapy) dogs, banned from visiting our families. It was my first insight into the real role of a dog, that of carer. And a shock to discover four legs a handicap. You can lie on the sofa all day long, but can you make your beloved a cup of tea?

Simon and his dogs are listed as one of the top sights in Greenwich.

19ᵗʰ June

No class last night. TD was that busy with work she forgot all about it, so now it's her fault if I misbehave.

20ᵗʰ June

I'd already been measured for the uniform when my life as a sniffer dog came to an abrupt halt.

Mrs King sat on her hotline, reporting an oddly-dressed man with strange hands, walking down our road with obvious ill intent. When five police cars raced to the scene of the imminent crime, they met an elderly gentleman in a cashmere coat and leather gloves on his way to post a letter. Mrs King has been stripped of her powers and cautioned over wasting police time.

Well, she may no longer be our neighbourhood watch co-ordinator, but the curtains in our road continue to twitch. Should anyone wonder where Mrs King lives, I'd say follow your nose. The smell of boiling cabbage will take you there.

27ᵗʰ June

Oh please, let sleeping dogs lie. The phone rang at some ungodly hour, wrecking my sleep. Not any old kip; your actual Stage Four Delta Brain Wave sleep, crucial for lowering my cortisol levels, melatonin and muscle repair. I might have drifted back except for the voice at the other end, both masculine and high-pitched, but not one of the Bee Gees. This was Aunt Annette over from the depths of Derry.

'Jane, have to see a property in Margate. You know Margate?' We sure knew Margate. It was my old stamping ground. I opened one eye.

'Must get in first before some other blighter grabs it.'

'Really?' said TD, taking a swig of coffee. 'Hang on, I've got an idea.'

'Oh! Super-duper. Spit it out.'

'How about a joint adventure: picnic, house-hunting and a chance for Dougal to see his family again?' Quick thinking, TD. I was now fully awake.

'Brilliant, brilliant Jane. See you in a tick. Oh, and I'll bring the picnic. You can always depend on me. PS, in case you're wondering, I'm looking for a second home.' The phone went dead.

'Annette, you're always looking for a second home, but you never make your mind up.' Had TD lost her senses? She was talking to the receiver. I stuck my head under my paws, hoping for REM sleep. Fat chance!

Bang. The front door shook. 'I hope you're prepared,' said TD, opening the door. After the force of that knocker, I sure was. In strode a woman, fuelled by more adrenalin than found in a pack of wolves.

'Jane, I'm here!' We could both see that. 'Hello, you

hairy mutt. Woof, woof, woof.'

Imagine how she's talks to the Christmas turkey!

'Woof, woof, Dougal, woof.' Of course I joined in and of course the noise levels increased. Within five minutes, Annette was prostrate with exhaustion and I was running around like a headless chicken.

We piled into Annette's shooting brake, the filthiest car I'd ever seen with oodles of boot room. Perfect for a bit of shut-eye, or so I thought. We kangaroo-hopped down our road, careered round the corner smack into a keep-left post and ricocheted back on to the pavement, missing the bus queue by a cat's whisker. I shot from one end of the car to the other, crashing into the door handle, badly injuring my quadriceps. The line of cars behind us beeped furiously. The pedestrians screamed blue murder.

'Annette, watch out!' We were hurtling perilously close to a van. Impact was inevitable. TD slammed on the handbrake, averting a collision.

'Please, take care! You're driving on a busy London road, not some remote Irish lane.'

'Bloody male drivers.'

'Annette, this is sheer hell.' I couldn't have agreed more. How come TD allowed her aunt anywhere near the wheel?

'Arseholes!' bellowed Annette, sticking two fingers out of the window.

'We're going to be lynched, if you carry on like this.' Half the world was clamped to their horns, the rest to their mobiles, calling the police. I lay down, hoping to be invisible.

'I've always dreamt of being a rally driver.' Annette jammed her foot hard on the accelerator and off we roared, pushing the poor old engine to its limits. If Annette thought she was in Brands Hatch, she was ten miles out – which is where a satnav helps. We'd escaped, or had we? Was our number plate really too dirty to read?

'Golly, that was fun. Now, I've brought a gourmet picnic. Where on earth did I put it?' Annette turned round to look.

'Please concentrate on driving.' TD was practically

begging her.

'Did I mention we need a service?'

'No, I don't think you…'

'Got to fill up every thirty miles.' We stopped almost immediately. 'Sweeties for Monty.' Annette collected four litres of oil. After the speed we'd been going, it should have been six.

'Perhaps you need a new car?' TD tentatively asked.

'Can't be parted; bought for Roy. Poor old love pegged out before he'd had the pleasure.'

'Sorry! What? Mind the van!'

'All was not lost. Drove his coffin to the funeral so he'd enjoy the experience first-hand, didn't we, Monty?' She patted the dashboard fondly.

Was TD listening to a word she said?

'Look, Jane, look over there! Don't you adore Friesian cows?'

'You must let me take over.'

Annette's body was hanging out of the window, the car driving itself. I shut my eyes and prayed. Would she come to her senses? I'd heard of elephants in dining rooms, but a cow in a car? Fortunately, Annette read my mind and our journey continued. As we jerked and swerved our way along the M2, I realised sleep was the least of my worries; staying alive was what mattered.

And arrive we did, without any dents to our car or others, even being shot at, knifed, or pulled over by the police. A miracle, if you ask me. St Christopher was doing a grand job.

In Margate I had an ecstatic reunion with my foster mother, Sally, and siblings Winston and Prue. Meaning, I was a total pain showing off my circus skills. While the others went house-hunting we were booted out to play in the garden. Before we'd turned the lawn into a complete bog they were back, excited, exhausted, no decision taken.

'I love it, just love it!' Annette was incapable of speaking quietly.

'But it is rather large,' suggested TD.

'No probs, I'll fill it with students.'

'But Annette…'

'No. No. I know exactly what I'll do. I'll sleep on it. When I wake I'll have the answer.'

Carrying the coolbox, we crossed the road to a large sandy beach, empty except for a few families, many seagulls and the odd dog. The sea was rough, the wind cold. TD wore coat, scarf and gloves. She always overdoes things.

'How thrilling! I can't smell the sea without diving in.' Annette tossed her jacket down on the wet sand. At least one of us had balls.

'But it's freezing.'

'Not for us Christmas Day swimmers.'

'And besides we haven't a towel or costume.'

I was up for a swim.

'Why argue with a woman who wore shorts to her own February wedding?' TD commented to Sal.

'I can provide a towel,' said Sally, helpfully. 'As for a costume…?'

'What on earth's underwear for?' That woman had a way of shouting the strong winds couldn't buffer. Every bird, man and beast turned to watch as she peeled down to her undergarments, hurled herself in and ploughed through the waves, three enthusiastic labradoodles in tow. I hadn't swum before but, unlike heel training, I didn't need lessons. And, unlike heel training, the experience was thrilling.

We'd barely shaken our coats free of water before Sally was back, running down the beach waving a bathrobe.

'I don't believe in all this fumbling under the towel nonsense,' Annette declared.

'Thank goodness the beach is empty.' TD averted her eyes as her naked aunt stood tall in her six-foot frame, drying herself. If only Annette had been a dog.

'Let's dig in. I'm famished.' Me too: she got that right.

The six of us stood round the coolbox, drooling in anticipation, but the picnic proved a huge disappointment: two carrots, six cocktail sausages, one small tomato and a slice of Victoria sponge.

'Oh, ample sufficiency; we'll be full to bursting.' How could such a large woman have such a small appetite?

'I think I'll fetch some more.' Good old Sal was back in a flash with enough food for a crowd, including dogs.

'I'm quite exhausted,' Annette announced to the company at large. Good grief! I'd barely blinked and it was time to go.

'I'll drive.' Thank god for TD; that owner of mine can be such a star. Sleep Annette did and, except for the noise of her snoring, it was a quiet run home. After one final stop – further treats for the wretched car – I stuck my head down hoping stage four sleep would repair my damaged muscles.

Once home, Annette fair bounced out of the car. 'Must pop in for a pee. OK if I use your lav?' She rushed in, rushed out. 'Great day, great day, must dash, can't keep the gang waiting.' Then, wielding a handkerchief, she skipped out of the door. Since Roy's death, she'd taken up Morris dancing. Which, as TD said, was pretty gutsy for a woman in her eighties, and especially hard if you have two left feet. A fact I hadn't noticed.

I have to admit, I am forever indebted to Annette. Thanks to her, I found my true identity. I may not be a water sign, but I am a water dog.

8ᵗʰ July

It was the perfect piggy-in-the-middle picture moment – missed naturally. It could have been sold to dog magazines. I might have been on YouTube. Me, stretched out on the sofa, TD and Mrs King squeezed at either end, hands in mouths voting for Andy Murray.

The atmosphere so tense you could cut it with a cleaver. We were all shouting at the players, only I was barking. I couldn't believe their incompetence; the double faults and unreturned serves. I could have caught those balls with ease and they had huge rackets.

Do the players know their game can get too exciting to watch? Well, it can and that's when people flee. Suddenly I was alone on the sofa, gripped but silent. The others were in the kitchen, door ajar, hoping to hear the words, 'Game, Set and Match to Murray.' If they so much as looked at the screen, Federer was bound to win. Such is the power of negative thought. They didn't watch. He still lost.

Next morning I was out in that park nicking every ball in sight, obsessed. Yep, overnight I found balls and lost all my dog friends, except for Tiger and Chester. The human ones I'd keep. I would need some mug to throw it. Not TD, she doesn't count.

I can truly say, paw on heart, Wimbledon changed my life.

9th July

It was our final class: the chance to show off our new-found tricks, get a certificate and say goodbye. We missed it.

The reason I didn't attend was simple. TD bottled out. She hadn't put the work in.

I was clueless about high-five, roll over or give us your paw. It would have shown her up.

Words fail me. It's time I faced facts. Not all heroes are super.

11th July

The sad news is Mrs King is leaving, going to live with her son, Martin, in Spain. It'll be good for her asthma, but I shall miss her and our TV dinners. Ivana is coming instead. She is from Croatia, dabbles in the occult and fears witches. Do we honestly want her living next door?

16th July

On this morning of my six-month birthday, I awoke with one thought in mind: not to hump Chester ever again.

23rd July

While the rest of the dog world suffers, thanks to my kennel cough vaccine, I'm alive and kicking. The park will be empty. Who shall I find to throw my ball?

Need to erase previous sentence before anyone reads it. I was being uncharacteristically selfish. I want to wish all sick dogs a speedy recovery.

There ought to be a Get Well card for dogs or, better still, an annual Pet Day. If Father's Day is some new invention by *Hallmark*, they're missing a major moneymaking opportunity with us pets. Forget about fish: they wouldn't remember.

6th August

Usain Bolt runs faster than squirrels, probably faster than whippets and is a damned sight faster than me. I'm enjoying the Olympics.

8th August

Not the slightest bit interested in dressage, but showjumping, that's different. As a natural jumper I applaud their skills. We were down in Greenwich ambling past the Queen's House, listening to the cheering crowds, hoping to catch a verse of the National Anthem, when it struck me: why not watch it live? I could sneak in through the playpark, wriggle my way to the front row and sit alongside the VIPs. If caught on camera, I'd only be put down as further evidence of *G4*'s incompetence. Sadly, my paws were tied. I was on the lead and a dream it would have to remain.

11th August

I shall live and die a pirate dog!

Heave Ho, Me Hearties! It was Jacob's fifth birthday and my first party invitation. The parents were hesitant, Jacob insistent.

'But what if he misbehaves or scares the children?' they asked their child. What four-year-old can promise to control a large puppy? But, as he said and the parents were bound to agree, he was about to be five and it was his party.

At 2 p.m. came the assault. Kitted out in hats, coats, boots and wielding enormous swords, a screaming horde of pirates invaded the party with a one-eyed dog in tow. Whatever I lacked in costume was compensated by wild enthusiasm. I threw myself into the role, terrifying the children as I pillaged and plundered the bounty: the birthday cake, sandwiches, sausages and trifle. Foods on my wish list. All on the forbidden list.

The parents said never, ever again. Word got out. It was my first and last children's party. It's so unfair. I'm still being trained and my sugar addiction is entirely Mrs King's fault.

14th August
I haven't humped Chester for four whole weeks. It wasn't a case of self-restraint. He's left London and gone to live in Kent. Tiger is now my only friend. Who says dogs don't feel guilt?

I've been banned from Putney. Hannah and Luke have had a garden makeover and bought two white sofas. I've never seen their house, so what's all that about?

20th August
I'm continuing to be a pain, handing my ball to all and sundry, especially babies in pushchairs. My ball carries germs and their mothers don't like it. OK, but the babies do, and anyway, aren't we meant to be encouraging the young to take up sport? I consider my ability with balls to be a singular talent – goodness knows, I've put the work in.

I empathise with Lang Lang, not that my father was as strict as his; in fact I have no memory of my father at all – but that's another story. Should anyone argue the genius theory, the naturally gifted versus hours of training, I'd tell them to look at Henry Moore's statue in Greenwich Park, great for cocking one's leg against, and ask how many hours of practice he clocked up during his student days.

31st August
Whatever happened? Did I get out the wrong side of bed or was it her? From the start nothing went right. TD forgot my

cup of tea, snack, water even, then we pavement-walked – mercifully I had the strength – to Alan, my vet, always a treat. Said hello to nurse Amber, then before I knew it, I was in the consulting room with a needle in my leg and out for the count. Not a Russian dissident, so nothing lethal. I awoke and oh, the pain! Couldn't think, couldn't walk. I was bashing against walls like a remote-controlled car in the hands of a two-year-old.

Finally got collected: along with pills, potions and a lampshade. Too ill to be left alone or lie on the floor. Three days' rest prescribed – Beaumont Beds is my dream break. If matters could get worse, TD had only booked a girlie weekend away, so I'm off to Kent, to stay with siblings. How on earth were the 'no walks or jumping-up' rules going to work? Some organisation on her part and they call me barking mad!

Next day, I travelled down the M20, head glued to rear window, wearing the dreaded lampshade. TD said if I thought of it as an Elizabethan ruff, I'd feel better. Let her wear one. No wonder they went out of fashion. Children in the cars behind waved and laughed. As I lay down to escape their mirth, my eyes drifted south and spotted a missing object. The radio played. Contralto voices of a Handel opera soared over the growl of the diesel engine. Heavenly melodies. I was in hell. I'm a knowledgeable beast, *au fait* with music, particularly the classical stuff, *Radio 3* keeping me company when home alone, hence well briefed in the countertenor and history of castrati.

My sperm-producing factory had gone. If I had sex, I wouldn't even be shooting blanks. I nosedived into the darkest melancholy, wallowing in self-pity. Then I remembered my mate, Tiger, who'd bravely suffered the same humiliation. I was resolved to stay strong for him. In order to face the world, minus malice and mockery, I pulled myself up on my shaky pins and solemnly swore, never, ever, to bark again. No one would catch me hitting a top A. Oh yes, suddenly it all made sense. I'd never heard Tiger bark.

Is TD aware of the neutered poodle and Addison's disease connection? If I die, she will never forgive herself. Had I stayed in bed, none of this would have happened. The lampshade has been renamed by *PIXAR The Cone of Shame*. *PIXAR* has to be a dog who suffered like me.

Nurse Amber runs a petting service. Why didn't I go there? Was ever there a dog more in need of TLC?

I got it wrong, misread the card. Amber runs a pet-sitting service, not a petting service. More's the pity.

2ⁿᵈ September

It's time I grew up. TD sat me down and told me she had exciting news to impart. I'm expecting a cousin. It's to live with Hannah and Luke. Luke has never had a dog before, not as an adult, not as a child. He grew up petless. When he shops, he has one criterion: WWHPD, which translates as What Would Harry Potter Do? Forget labradoodles, far too muggle-like. A sleek black hound is on order.

Being older, I'm to show it the ropes. Will I step up to the plate? And can this really be credited as exciting news?

3ʳᵈ September

Advice for dogs of all ages – I'm going to get a kick out of this.

Don't grab treats if you want another. You are not a crocodile.

Suck it and see. Frozen foods are best defrosted.

Take no notice of the five-second ruling. Eat all food lying on pavements. Never adhere to sell-by dates.

Oh yes, almost forgot. Never crap on Platform 3 at Charing Cross station.

6ᵗʰ September

Up with the crows! Luckily my early morning fragility is improving with age. We're driving Mrs King to Gatwick and collecting Ivana. An airport run and a new route to get to grips with – quite excited by the prospect.

We returned with Ivana, who talks nineteen to the dozen

and is more impossible to understand than a toothless Mrs King. No wonder we got lost, in Croydon of all godforsaken places. I guess someone has to live there. This wasn't a good day for my satnav skills. As for the traffic going, surprised anyone catches their plane.

10th September
Back to see Alan, the man responsible for my male genital mutilation, hence my greeting was cool. Before I had the chance to dash out of the door, I found myself flat on my back, legs in air, being prodded and poked. Indignities pregnant dogs frequently endure, so tried to remain stoic.

'Ah,' said TD, peering at my sac, 'looks like a handbag.'

'True,' agreed Alan, 'an empty one.' Who'd be a dog? Were I human, I'd have my hand in a box of Cadbury creams. It'll take months for my relationship with Alan to heal.

12th September
I must have made a real hit with Annette on our Margate trip; she's having a break from cats – yes, she owns one, too – and has offered to walk me when TD's busy. How will she cope with an energetic young hound? She'll be my oldest dog walker by half a century.

15th September
Latest info on new arrival: Ivana fears the colour black and wears her slip inside-out to ward off evil. How does TD know this? If black upsets the lady, why smoke Sobranie cigarettes and what happens at funerals? Mrs King would have made it her business to find out.

20th September
Absolutely whacked! Two whole hours spent catching cricket balls bowled at the speed of light.

'Get this one, Dougal!' 'Good one, boy!' 'No, you dunderhead, you don't need a pee.' And oh, my teeth! Try fielding those balls without any headgear. Did Annette imagine she was bowling for England? Twenty overs later, I collapsed and had to be carried off the pitch. Cricket is a terrifying game.

TD tells me Annette, who'd spent her first nine years of life in her father's prep school hurling cricket balls at a hundred miles an hour, was desperate to check if she'd lost her knack. I can tell her right now, she hasn't.

30th September

Been earwigging; catching snippets of Cockney Rhyming Slang, a fun secret language, much of it involving food. Apples and Pears, Raspberry Tart, Dog and Bone. My stomach rumbles as I listen out for more.

Since there aren't any phrase books or any Adult Ed classes on the subject, getting the hang of it may prove hard. Once deciphered – surely easier to crack than a Bletchley Park code – I'll weave it into my daily vocab.

2nd October

When I heard it was raining cats and dogs, I received the news with mixed emotions. Thrilled at the thought of cats dropping out of the sky and horrified over those panic-stricken dogs plunging to their death. I wanted to cry.

This is where cats and their nine lives win every time over dogs. I imagine they abseiled gracefully down.

8th October

Today, the *Daily Telegraph* announced Seven Black Labrador Puppies born to delighted breeders, Poppet and Chubby Paget. Hannah and Luke have bagged a boy. He will arrive in December, not by post. Do they know a dog is for life, not just for Christmas? And why did they buy white sofas, when they were about to get a black puppy? I should have compiled a 'do and don't' list for them.

Annette has booked a flight to Oz, so won't be spending Xmas with us. I must wait another year to find out what she says to the turkey.

10ᵗʰ October

You'd think they were expecting a baby. Amazon is so busy transporting parcels to Putney they are running short of drivers.

So far the puppy has no name. Luke wants to call him Fangs, after Hagrid's dog. Hannah says it's a horrid name for a toothless, two-day-old puppy.

14ᵗʰ October

We were meeting Hannah in Barnes, not for the Boat Race – that we missed months ago. It was a blisteringly hot day and the towpath was heaving with families making the most of the weather. Next month, London will be battening down the hatches, jumping into thermals and vegetating for the winter – a human habit caught from squirrels.

We sped along the tow path, river to one side, trees and back gardens on the other, dodging bikes, pushchairs and runners. They did, I didn't.

'Dougal, mind the baby. Oh, sorry, so sorry! Dougal!' I was high as a kite, charging through the dried leaves, my tail going like the clappers, as I sniffed dogs, chased cats and greeted every toddler going. Then, from the other side of the wall came the sounds of oars dipping in and out of the water, male voices, cries and laughter. The river was brimming with fun. I had to join in. With one Olympian leap, I was over.

Bonkers Dougal! Never underestimate the consequences of your actions. The water was only twelve metres below. Did I shimmy down the walls? No way. I dropped, one furry bundle of panic in free fall, my life vanishing behind me, the Thames looming ever closer, when a ledge, barely large enough to house a seagull, interrupted my descent. By some miracle, I was able to grip. Thank the Lord I'd never had my nails cut.

From somewhere above me, I heard familiar voices shouting, 'Dougal!'

I just managed to keep my footing and look up. The two bodyless heads of TD and Hannah appeared over the wall.

'Don't move!' they yelled in unison. My six puppy classes had had an effect. I obeyed. 'Dougal, we're going for help. Stay still.' Now, Alan, my vet, may call me pea-brained, but on this occasion, some grey matter functioned. I tried dwelling on my circus heritage. Hang about, were poodles used in high-wire acts? Dougal, just focus, you fool. Think of agility, precision and balance. If one toe faltered, I'd be down that wall and carted off in the current. If dogs could sob!

'Dougal.' They must have heard me whimpering. 'Be brave, Dougal. Keep calm.' Calm! If no one came to my aid, I'd be a goner.

Suddenly, three heads appeared. TD's, Hannah's and one belonging to a little old lady who'd arrived with a pile of old sheets and the number of the river police.

'We're going to tie these together and pull you up.' Was I really expected to cling on to a sheet with my teeth? My future was not looking rosy. I imagined my funeral: park mates and grieving family. What music would they chose? Handel – no chance! Madagascar's *Move it, move it* – possible. *I'll do it my way* – much more like it. Of course, I'd miss out on the pub grub. And how much would she put behind the bar?

'Get a grip, Dougal,' I told myself. 'You can't give up the ghost that easily.'

Ghosts! Were there dog ghosts? Did I possess a soul? And if so would I eject it from my body on impact of death, contact Ivana next door and have D O U G A L spelt out on her ouija board – even return in my next life as a black cab driver and use my satnav skills. I'd already done The Knowledge.

Whoops, I had almost lost my footing. My legs were dissolving to jelly. Help! Hanging on was becoming nigh impossible. The river would claim me, my corpse wash up on a bank for TD to identify. If she had me stuffed for posterity, where would I sit? I was too big for the piano.

'Dougal! Dougal!' They were calling my name. I was back in the real world, my heart beating at a terrifying rate, screaming for beta-blockers.

I counted four heads hanging over the wall. A jogger had joined the party and was busily recruiting others. Before I fully absorbed this fact, he, followed by not one but two runners, bombed over the parapet, transformed their bodies into a chain of young male muscle and grabbed me by the collar. As quickly as it had started, my ordeal was over.

My hero was then pulled to safety. He'd only risked his life for me.

'God, I need a drink!' said Hannah.

'We need wine,' agreed TD. And off to a pub we went. This time I was on the lead.

I now realise my existence to be a blessing. Henceforth I shall treasure every moment of it. Meanwhile, I'm going to say a big thank you to my rescuer.

Metro 16.10.2012
GOOD DEED FEED Text **DEED** followed by your comment
Name and where you live to **65400**

Thank you to the young man who pulled me back from the brink of death on the towpath in Barnes on Sunday, endangering his own life. You are my knight in shining armour.

A very big lick from your furry friend, DOUGAL. SE London.

If we are interviewed on national TV, I'd prefer *The One Show*. Should I be tempted to jump over that same section of wall, I shall remind myself I'm not a lemming.

18th October
Although we meet Andy and Tiger each morning, I only have eyes for my ball. Thanks to the addiction I have dropped all dog friends. Because of my op, I've lost most physical sensation. Should I be worried?

20ᵗʰ October

Further puppy advice or, rather, indoor entertainment for dogs of all ages.

Don't get out of bed if the shipping forecast's on.

Farming Today is worth staying awake for. As for *The Archers* – don't get me started. It's gone right downhill lately. Too many family problems, too few farming stories and the animal noises are at a record low. And what's happened to the hundreds of voice-over artists? I mean, do these animals belong to a union? You can bet your life they don't sign on. I shall put in a complaint to the head of *Radio 4*.

Been wracking my brain for further pearls. Sadly, wisdom doesn't come easily.

26ᵗʰ October

I have often wondered: are children born scared of dogs? Are dogs born terrified of fireworks, or do the parents encourage our paranoia? For here we are fast approaching the most dreaded date on the calendar for pets and owners.

Bonfire Night is an ancient ritual, involving the burning of an effigy of a guy named Guy, who, unlike Pocahontas, didn't get saved. There used to be thousands of these Guy dummies sitting on street corners or outside supermarkets, making a fast buck before they got burnt. Then the government intervened. Supposedly, it sent out confusing messages. If it was acceptable for a child to burn a straw man dressed in their dad's pyjamas, they might think it OK to burn their dad, if he told them off, grounded them or something. So now the burning of all effigies is out and Bonfire Night usually happens without them. It's all rather confusing, but that's my take on it.

27ᵗʰ October

The new subject for discussion is pills. Which is cheaper: *Boots* or *Pets at Home*? Does human medication work for dogs? Is homeopathy worth a try or would it only succeed for Prince Charles?

31st October

Few days left. Brief respite as Halloween shifts the focus. We're indoors in the dark hiding from Trick or Treaters, pretending to be out when actually we are in. If it's a case of treats versus rotten eggs, why not give 'em all a box of chocolates?

'Then we'll have the whole of London round,' argues TD. How does she know if she's never tried it? Can the capital really be that desperate for a Roses chocolate? This is a prime example of the half-empty view on life.

1st November

If the whole world's got issues, I want one. Titch has anger issues, Tiger anxiety ones and now Jacob's developed a maths issue.

So what about me? Where are mine? I'm missing out here.

3rd November

Today's the day of the large display and panic has returned big time. Whilst most dogs are at home listening to desensitizing music, my mates Titch and Tiger will be freaking out. Titch beneath a duvet on PAH meds and Tiger treating the coffee table as an air raid shelter, in earmuffs and on giant-sized pills – enough to make a mouse sleep for a month, the vet informed Andy. As a dog immune to loud noises, I remain drug-free.

9 p.m.

What an experience! First a speedy run round the block, to double-check my noise threshold, then off to the display we headed. Along roads packed with happy children, all waving sparklers, then on to the Heath. I lay on the damp grass with a small child on top of me, watching fireworks dropping from the sky. The few dogs we bumped into were all black Labs. The bangs were a breeze. Was more concerned over the flashing lights. If I've caught epilepsy, I'll need a brain scan.

To be honest, the noise sounded worse when indoors. Perhaps all dogs should go to the firework display. On second thoughts, bad idea – with that many legs, we'd be crushed to death.

4th November. 8 a.m.

Back in park. Thanks to smog, visibility poor. The few dogs we came across looked bleary-eyed; most were probably still in bed, groggy from medication. If this was done to humans, the country would grind to a halt.

The fun's not over yet. The official day being tomorrow. November the fifth is Uncle John's birthday. He will be eighty-nine – around six hundred and twenty-three in dog years. He is a keen pyro-technician. TD has a friend who does fireworks on a grand scale: the Olympics, Queen's Jubilee – a busy summer. This was not Uncle John. He is untrained. Uncle John has firework displays on his roof, near Russell Square, glass of plonk in one hand, lit fag in other, excellent for igniting rockets. Now that does sound like fun. He will be ninety next year. It's bound to be a special event. Roll on 2013. If it turns out I'm epileptic, I shan't be able to attend.

7th November

Below I have listed dog-friendly places where food is donated.

Most butchers allow you in and give you bones.

Cats Protection League hand out treats – no, not cats.

Pubs prefer dogs to children. Titbits include crisps, biscuits and the occasional beer.

If this puppy refuses to heed my advice, my efforts will have been wasted.

I'm still refusing to hand TD my ball. I like to think of it as giving other folk equal ops. TD says I'm OCD and getting a ball off me is comparable to pulling teeth.

8th November

Hannah and Luke have visited the puppies and picked their

boy. They have fallen in love. He is the cutest, sweetest, softest... I want to be sick. TD says my nose is out of joint. There's nothing wrong with my nose.

Their Baby, as they call him, is a fifth-generation gun dog. Both his parents hunt and fish. This is impossible in Putney High Street. And the deer in Richmond Park are not for shooting. Does Luke know this?

9th November

The words Libran and Capricorn are being bandied about. Haven't heard of horoscopes but shall look into them.

When I learnt I was sharing my body with a billy goat, I wished I hadn't. I knew I had something stored inside, but hadn't expected anything that substantial. As a Capricorn, my path is to understand the needs of others, which is what dogs do, so no revelations there. But as I read on, it says we're sure-footed and thoroughly practical. In the end the Capricorn always reaches the heights, beating others who are faster but less determined – me to a T with a ball. It also states I have strong white teeth and am conscious about my appearance. How true.

Librans (the puppy's sign) are handsome, elegant and likened to a finely-tuned wind instrument, producing powerful, moving music in perfect harmony. God help me!

Add to this: the terror of being alone, sulky, extremely intelligent and gullible! Having a sense of fair play is his one redeeming feature.

I'm digging in my heels, refusing to give the little sod any further advice. Jacob can't wait to meet him. He's going to love this puppy better than me, I just know it.

10th November

From its swinging, toe-tapping start, the day deteriorated rapidly. Now I'm all hot and bothered. My cousin, barely four weeks old, is texting his new family on a daily basis, and sending pics. This is me doing high five. Today, I slept for twenty hours. What I'd like in my new nursery. I mean, come on! At that age I could barely think, let alone text. I can't even do it now. He'll be tweeting next or getting his own Facebook page.

The name Fangs has been dropped. *Kennel Club* didn't approve.

11th November

Today, I seriously misjudged the situation and pushed my luck. I asked a stranger to throw my ball, dropping it politely at his feet. An offer he accepted twice, but balked third time round, saying he resented being treated like a slave. TD says my obsession with balls is a real issue.

So that's it, I've got them: issues, ball issues, major ones. Fab; love it! I've finally made the grade.

12th November

Bad month for morale! Should people be allowed to air their jaundiced views?

'Oh, you've bought a rug.' 'Stick him in the washing machine.' This morning got told I look like an old man with a cigar. I'm ten months old.

They keep saying I'm getting there. Wherever *there* is, I haven't reached it yet.

One is going to be my perfect age.

17th November

TD says she's over the hill. Really! It was her birthday, a pub event so I could join in. And join in I did – excessively.

'Oh, it's harmless,' cried Ian, a man, who has beer coursing through his veins and is in the know.

'Or like champagne parties, when waiters come round topping you up, before you've got to the bottom and you never know how much you've drunk.' How right TD was. There came that point in the evening when we were both hammered and Ian ordered us a taxi. Few cabbies choose to drive an inebriated woman accompanied by her drunken dog. Ian must have bribed him. I was legless and having four non-working legs is decidedly worse than two. There's no way could I have made it to the bus.

46

TD's friends have been sworn to secrecy. If the *RSPCA* hears about my binge drinking, I could get taken away which wouldn't be fair. TD had no idea I was being administered alcohol. At least it wasn't snakebite.

The pub is getting a new sign. **No alcohol to be served to anyone under the age of 18, including dogs.** Although I've taken the pledge, I believe if a dog gets to eighteen, it deserves a free shandy.

20th November

The puppy story gets worse. This babe of barely six weeks is already toilet-trained.

When he gets collected in two weeks' time I bet he won't jump up, chew, fall into the Thames or get covered in mud. Jealousy may be an unattractive quality, but I'm beginning to hate this ball of soot and we haven't even met. Arguments over his name continue.

22nd November

Going for a pedicure; returning to the man I no longer trust, Alan.

Am I a pushover when offered liver treats or did I forget my promise? Whichever. I melt faster than marshmallows in a cup of hot chocolate the second we meet. I have to accept it; Alan will always have the upper hand.

25th November

Dear Diary, humans are mad and can't tell the time.

How could I be so naïve? We woke late, breakfasted before the walk, which sure messed up my digestive system, not to mention my routine. TD put on skirt, backpack and stuck me in my harness (pavement-walking gear). Yep, I should have picked up the signs. Then off we trotted across the Heath. Not a second to sniff, cock a leg, let alone... whoops, past the pond, ducks, geese and seagulls. Down the hill, we rushed into the station and on to a train full of dog-allergic children, friends visiting museums, Planet Hollywood, Hamleys and Buckingham Palace but not the

Queen. Shame: she likes corgis, so might like seven-year-olds. Mind, if they didn't like dogs, she probably wouldn't.

At Waterloo, we changed to a different line and were struggling along a crowded platform when a stranger stopped us. 'Oh look, fluffy dog. Does he bite?' Do I look as if I bite?

What, no trains to Putney? It's Clapham Junction and a replacement bus. 'Oh, bugger that,' said TD. She's prone to swearing.

Change of plan? Home, I hoped. No such luck. Off to the tube, miles below ground and no lift at this mainline station. What if I were wheelchair-bound? Lucky the *Transport for London* guys were helpful.

'Think you'll find escalator No 10 out of action. Will he be OK using that?' Come on, what sort of idiot did they take me for? On to the Jubilee Line we went. No dog-haters but bursting with Christmas shoppers or families off to Winter Wonderland. It was hell on earth and the only time I wished I'd been born a teacup Chihuahua, the perfect handbag pet. I crammed myself into a corner, surrounded by legs, bikes and umpteen suitcases heading for Heathrow. I knew the routine: don't sleep against the doors. They may suddenly open and you either fall out or get squashed in the stampede. And, watch your butt, else as sure as dammit an announcement will burst through the loudspeaker: 'Doors failing to close; large blond tail causing obstruction.'

When eventually we arrived, Hannah was nowhere to be seen. She differs from a labradoodle and is not a meet and greet girl. We headed for her house, knocked, no answer. Heck, we'd come all this way and no one was in. So now I, the non-verbal dog, broke down and cried. Well, actually, I bleated. Before I'd the chance to recover we were off retracing our steps at the speed of a racing greyhound, when across the road, engulfed in coffee fumes, I spotted her. Having zero road sense, we crossed the busy Putney High Street with utmost caution. And there, at long last, I was able to jump up and say hello.

We pavement-walked to Barnes, met friend Sharon from

Glasgow who has a way with dogs but is impossible to comprehend. Then off the four of us went to the Farmers' Market with its stalls perfectly arranged at nose height. Before my tongue could wipe the tables clean of pork pies and fairy cakes, I was tied to the gate and forced to watch the local dogs, old Labs too long in the tooth to bother with food, waddle round this canine paradise.

Without any warning, the heavens opened. Rain is a human allergy, similar to peanuts but not as severe. 'Let's take refuge at the Sun Inn,' they all cried. This was the best idea yet. Here I wasn't just welcomed but fed Gloucester Old Spot sausage, patted, stroked and thoroughly indulged.

Twelve long hours later, after an exhausting day being photographed by Japanese tourists, trodden on by strangers, given treats by Sharon, plus all the hours of travel on two trains, four tubes, two escalators, three lifts and one bus, when we finally arrived home I was too cream-crackered to eat.

Just got wind of tomorrow's plans: we're back in town, seeing Uncle John. It's my first smart luncheon invitation, so shall need to impress. Now this warrants very careful consideration. If people imagine my appearance doesn't matter, they couldn't be more wrong, as evident from my *Match.com* profile – still at the planning stage.

GSOH
Size – medium (skinny isn't sexy)
Height – medium (most men lie)
Shaggy – nice way of saying scruffy
Blond – no bombshell but can brush up well
High IQ – not always apparent
Famous – in Greenwich Park
Hobbies – all ball games, indeed, much in common with our famous mayor. But unlike Boris, who hires a team of Polish make-up artists to mess up his immaculate appearance, padding his stomach, loosening his belt and tousling his hair, generally beavering away till our man, chuffed with his appearance, shouts, 'Stop! I'm dishevelled enough.' I have

to go it alone.

I don't exactly have a wardrobe, more a choice of styles. There's the black tie, booted and suited, or dinner and dance as I prefer to think of it, the Titchmarsh, the Attenborough Experience and finally the Dalyan.

The Black Tie works well if the head, neck and chest are dunked in a large muddy hole. Picture a duck diving.

Booted and Suited requires a deeper muddy pool for its execution, that or digging up an herbaceous border.

The Alan Titchmarsh Look demands duckweed, snails, indeed, all pondlife. This style is great for camouflage and fancy dress parties.

For **the Attenborough Experience**: mud, sand, sticks, leaves and grass must be employed, plus all insects, dead or alive, the full eco-system.

And lastly, my proudest design to date, **the Dalyan Mud Bath**. This sublime beauty treatment, enjoyed by humans, hippos and now canines, is far cheaper than a flight to Marmaris. Once dry, the result is an exquisitely matted coat, similar to a hand-woven kilim. Useful as a thermal layer in winter, cooling in the summer and giving added protection against the worst of UV rays.

And there I have it: choices for all weathers, including a summer and winter range. For Uncle John, a black tie will do nicely. All I require is the right walk.

I overdid it and was left at home.

29ᵗʰ November
Annette has forgotten it'll be summer in Australia and she can't take the heat. She's off to Ireland, instead.

1ˢᵗ December
The decorations are up. Even as a Christmas novice, this seems far too early.

'Gets me in the mood,' she tells me. Whatever makes her happy, but the shopping levels are way over the top and we've still three weeks to go.

5ᵗʰ December

My cousin, now called Indy after Indiana Jones, has arrived with crate, toys and a framed pedigree certificate. He's being treated like royalty and his diet is something else. No, really, I can't believe my ears. Weetabix, poached eggs, Carnation milk, Ambrosia rice pudding with mince and a ton of biscuits; all adding up to a colossal 4,800 calories. He's not even six kilos. How heavy will he be next week?

Am sick to the back teeth hearing about the LB (little beast). Decided all this obsessing is having a negative effect on my naturally sunny nature.

7ᵗʰ December

Better day in park; comments more positive. 'Ho, ho, ho, he's been having fun.' 'Can see he loves life.' 'What a jolly dog!' Spirit's immediately on the up. It doesn't take much to cheer a simple soul like me.

11ᵗʰ December

Who are these Joneses we're keeping up with?

Our windows remind me of cars with tinted windows, except we cannot see out. For once I'm innocent. It's no inside job, no smear marks, nothing involving my nose. Road works are being blamed. We're getting a window cleaner, Dave, from Wales. We have met and I love him.

Further puppy news. Indy is doing better than well. He is not greedy. On that diet, how could he be? He has a high IQ. On that diet, how could he not have? He went to a puppy class. Note the A. Yes, one. Learnt everything and doesn't have to go back. Is this possible? I'm blaming my early London life for my low IQ. The lack of sleep and calories has had massive impact on my brain power.

12ᵗʰ December

Four men turned up when TD was out. I heard their ladders going up, the team spraying, wiping, rubbing and rattling the windows. I felt the need to protect my castle against this nice man named Dave and, temporarily forgetting the promise I'd made back in August, I barked for England. No top A, but beautiful baritone tones. I couldn't believe it, all those months of wasted worry.

When TD returned and was unable to open the door, she couldn't believe it. *Greenwich Locks* were called out and £81.60 later TD entered the house. By jumping up, I'd locked the door from inside.

I assumed TD would be thrilled I had finally found my voice. But no, she hadn't bought me as a guard dog and saw it as emptying the family coffers rather than adding to the global economy. Will we ever agree?

14th December

Could be this puppy wasn't the best of buys. He left his mother too early, is insecure, needs a pacifier and gets carsick. They're off to Cornwall for Xmas. Luke is driving. That'll be one fun journey.

16th December

Hannah and Luke brought their 'baby' over for tea. If this was to show him off, it didn't work. He peed all over the place, ate my food, then pooped on the carpet. House-trained? I don't think so. If you're cute you can get away with murder. I was cute, once.

Hannah say Indy will think the sun shines out of my arse, when he's older. Do I want him to?

17th December

It's my First Noel or Xmas Extravaganza, and life's about to go tits-up. Said farewell to all my park mates. For the foreseeable future our routines are liable to be disrupted as present shopping becomes a solitary venture. Forbidden to sit outside shops, even wait in the car. TD believes people are so desperate for money they might be pushed to steal even me. What a preposterous idea! As if I'd let them. It's Dougal the Labradoodle, we're talking about. I'm one stubborn hound.

18th December

The relentless shopping continues without let-up. Who is it all for? The spare room is chocka, with more packages stuffed through the letterbox whenever my back is turned. I am hoarse from barking at postmen.

I'm suffering from neglect. To compensate, have been allowed to lounge on the sofa in front of the telly. Am steadily working my way through the Xmas slush.

Beethoven – 6th viewing. *101 Dalmatians* – one of Jacob's favourites, so probably my 50th.

19th December

Think it might be Wednesday. Lost count of days. Now the presents are sorted, food shopping has begun in earnest. Cupboards are full, fridges bursting and cellar stacked to the gills. This is going to be some feast.

20th December

TD is back out buying. She's already on her knees and the festivities haven't begun.

Watched *Turner and Hooch* – 1st viewing. Such a relief to see dogs misbehave. I get so teed off watching perfect dog movies.

21st December

When I'm older I swear I shall write a book called *Family Life for Dummies*.

TD had a job plus Jacob, not the best combo, and, to crown it all, Miriam, my royal minder, had escaped to Bratislava, hence I was home, too.

Any Labrador would have loved it: pheasants roasting in the ovens, kitchen table awash with sprouts and the fridges brimming with unset jellies. The preparations were in full swing when Jacob dropped the bombshell: Father Christmas was sick, unable to deliver. The children of the world were waiting. It was a crisis and up to us to sort it.

With Jingle Bells blasting from the iPod, we flew into action. We required presents, an elf, Rudolf and a sleigh.

Old teddies spewed from the toy chest at volcanic speed as TD hung socks, large and small, ski and knee, on every door and every floor. A sledge rose from the cellar, then Alice band antlers were attached to my head.

In a loop-the-loop dash round the world in ten minutes, we needed a magic carpet, not some plastic blue sledge. Hauling gifts and an elf, we were off on our mission – to where, tell me, where? Were we in Sweden, Denmark or India? It was aching, back-breaking. Oh, for a breather, water and fuel.

But upstairs we struggled, flight after flight, huffing and puffing, posting crackers and toys, chocolate and fruit, across prairies and continents, never once stopping till all stockings were full. Then a shrill whistle blew. Break time at last? They piled the car high with the festive delights. One final delivery, to where did I care? I staggered to bed; was I ever pooped.

23rd December

Unable to move, slumped in front of TV all day long. Elves weigh a ton. After watching countless Santa films, I am now more wised-up on my Rudolf role. If yesterday is anything to go by, I'm dreading Christmas.

Meanwhile, she is cooking up a storm. Banned from kitchen as per usual, allowed to lie in doorway and observe. Just when I imagined settling down for a nice cosy cuppa, she cleaned the house from top to bottom and fetched a duster – not previously witnessed. Are we expecting the Queen?

Christmas Eve

We rose at some horrendously unhealthy hour, had no breakfast to speak of and certainly no walk. The only exercise was housework; something about floors being clean enough to eat off. That's a new one. No sooner had I thrown up my paws in a fit of adolescent pique, coachloads of friends burst through the door bringing goodies, babies and barrels of laughter. Wow! If this was Christmas, had I ever got it wrong?

After dinner, we walked to a church in Greenwich for an unrehearsed join-in-if-you-want-to Nativity play.

'I will, if you will,' said Jacob, so I did. Isn't a dog a boy's best friend?

'Choose a character, pick a costume from the box by the door, then come and see me.' A woman boomed orders from the other end of the church.

We all stood dutifully before her: twelve kings, ten shepherds (nine plus Jacob), eight Angel Gabriels, six inn-keepers, five Josephs, three Marys, one baby Jesus and a sheep, me. I was the whole flock. Had I been fatter, I might have been cast as the donkey and had a leading role taking Mary to Bethlehem.

Jacob and I sat in the aisle, nervously waiting for our cue. Would they shout *'Action,'* or call us more formally: Mr Jacob and Mr Dougal to the stage, please?

'Sheep and shepherds, go now, go!' yelled the same not-to-be-messed-with voice. What! It was us. Jacob grabbed me by the scruff of my neck and on we rushed with the other shepherds, ready to hear the Good News, instead scattering a horde of sobbing children, terrified of large dogs.

However, the story must go on and after a slight hiccup did, as the snivelling infants returned with their mums and dads, increasing the fold to forty-four children, thirty-four parents, two directors, one baby of three weeks plus its breast-feeding mother and me. All in all, more extras on this tiny stage at the foot of the altar than a 1960s MGM Blockbuster Jesus Movie.

I lay down as I would on a crowded train. The tears melted away and the story continued without interruption. The three-week-old baby was born again, and the kings and shepherds paid their respects. Once the show was over, the church transformed itself into one of those petting farms, except I was the only animal to pet.

Tired but elated, we made our way home for the children's bedtime. Jim-jams on, stories read and Santa sacks hung. What, no socks! At least I couldn't spoil Christmas Day by eating one. And finally, snacks were laid out beside the fireplace: mince pies and whisky for Father Christmas, a carrot for Rudolf. Do they both come down the chimney? Do reindeers really fly? I thanked my lucky stars we hadn't attempted that.

Christmas Day
Father Christmas had been and delivered. The real McCoy, except I never saw him, caught a whiff of reindeer or spotted any droppings.

A day of presents and delicious dishes stretched before us. And as I ate my way through piles of crisps, cheese straws, sausage rolls, turkey and stuffing, I knew my prayers had been answered. I was piling on the pounds.

What a day! What a party! Food, glorious food! I doubt the Queen's corgis had had a banquet like ours.

I spent the night in the garden. The change of diet had attacked the bowels.

26ᵗʰ December
Toddling round the block has been cleverly renamed the Boxing-Day walk. If it started badly, the disappointment of my day continued. For all the food that passed my lips, I could have had a *Nil by Mouth* sign hanging round my neck. Not for them: they pigged out and then, without so much as a by-your-leave or offer to clear up, vanished. Home had never seemed so quiet.

TD took one look at the chaos and poured herself a large gin. With that much mess to clear up, I'd have made it a triple. The party is well and truly over. It's back to normal, except it isn't; walks are short, tempers shorter. We've come off the high. I'm living with bi-polar. And we're broke – like stony. Twenty measly quid to last till the end of the month.

Just checked cellar: do have rations in food bin. Phew! Today is the day all puppies bought for Christmas, if they haven't already made it to Battersea, are in the bin.

I am resolved to be the perfect dog.

27th December
We vegged out! TD called it, 'having a duvet day'.

28th December
TD is no graduate of the Hoxton Circus School. Nevertheless, she spent hours in front of the bedroom mirror, juggling clothes, tape measures and scales. Swear words an optional extra, one she grabbed with both fists. The festivities have increased her waist measurements. Nothing fits. Buy larger ones, I'd say, or wear a corset. I lay patiently beside her, head on lap, trying to exude my inner karma.

But no. 'Life is going to change!' she screamed. 'Come Tuesday, the resolutions will begin.' I fear for her sanity.

31st December. New Year's Eve
Unsure whether to be pleased or vexed! TD woke up smiling, even began singing. Of course, I'm thrilled she's happy, but she's tone-deaf, hard on the ears of a dog that isn't. Tonight is the big celebration, the final blow-out of the year, before winter bites.

I'm home alone with the telly, two carrots and an apple. With that much 'sorry food', it's sure to be a late one.

1st January 2013
God alone knows what time she crawled in. Let's hope she didn't leave her wallet in the cab. Sure wouldn't be a first. Meanwhile, she slept through my walk, breakfast, and remainder of the day. Woke in one hell of a mood and then what? Well, not a lot.

A handful of pills later, she dived back under the duvet. The hangover has taken its toll, rendering New Year's Day a wash-out. At least I was given a large dinner.

2nd January. 11 a.m.
Not a load better. While the rest of the world returns to

work, TD remains in a vegetative state. All in all, two days of life lost.

3 p.m.
As I write this, she is soaking in a warm oiled bath, using all her Christmas gifts in one fell swoop. Due to sudden light sensitivity this is taking place by candlelight – a further expense. And the heating is on 24/7, like suddenly the bills don't matter. She'll regret her extravagance.

3rd January
Just when I'd believed her atrophied brain had deleted the D word forever, the South Beach Diet commenced. Two days late, the resolutions had begun.

4th January
Day one ended with no weight loss.

5th January
Day two, one pound down = low self-esteem. Surely a weekly weigh-in would limit the damage?

12 p.m.
It's extraordinarily how fragile the human race becomes when germs invade. TD has a blocked nose. Whenever she rummages in a pocket for hankies, she pulls out a poo bag. This is not helping her temper. Has her weight loss, small that it is, destroyed her immune system?

2.30 p.m.
TD fell off the wagon. Not yet Twelfth Night and all resolutions out of the window. On a new regime: cheese, chocolate and whisky – a wee dram, taken with pills. From where I was sitting, looked more like a pint.

6th January. My first Birthday!
Blocked sinuses, earache, catarrh, water streaming from

eyes, nose and mouth. Her head has turned into a snot-making machine. The only thing to dry up is my walk. Trips to the chemist for emergency medication are now our only outings. At the rate TD is emptying the shelves of Day and Night Nurse, stocks'll run dry. And I thought I'd cornered the hypochondria market.

We're celebrating my birthday when TD's better. Like the Queen, I shall have two: actual and official.

7th January

TD is going downhill fast. She hasn't moved from the sofa and sounds like a frog. The heating is on top whack. We're living in the tropics. Scratching constantly. TD believes I have fleas.

Am desperate to help, Battersea always lurks in the background. Not being a retriever or trained as a mobility dog, I'm struggling. Have managed to fetch one slipper, a box of tissues, Lemsip and an apple, which TD refused to eat as was covered in teeth marks. Allowed to finish it.

Her snoring is interrupting my sleep.

10th January

Behind with diary: too busy as a carer. Lack of exercise is compensated by constant companionship. I'm on the sofa, head on lap, enjoying a diet of daytime TV. We are now, officially, couch potatoes. One of my goals finally achieved.

Food programmes have been swapped for holiday destinations. Big relief. I thought if one more chef showed me how to stuff a turkey, I'd throw up. Actually, the safari ones are worth watching. It's good to know the cats in our garden are domestic.

11th January

The snoring has stopped, her additional weight, dropped. Spirits are lifting; she's on the mend. While TD ventured out alone, I caught up with some Me-Time – my new term for sleep.

Many hours later, she returned full of the joys, carrying a

tree's worth of paper with the result there's no space to swing a cat. Our home is littered with brochures – all exotic locations: Morocco, the shores of Mauritius and the ski slopes of Europe.

13ᵗʰ January

I'm in the flattest spin ever. We're getting away from it all. Seriously, I'm going, too. The human world is opening up to us hounds. There are bijou hotels and B&Bs where dogs are more indulged than their masters. I believe we're travelling by air. Being under two, I should go free and have my own seat. I need a passport. After my first jab, we're off.

TD is busy researching airline options. As it's my first flight, I am expecting to be spoilt. EasyJet or Ryanair – no way, you don't get lunch or a steward looking after you. Airline stewards are in my line of work – except they are your proper meet and greet guys.

I can't wait to introduce myself.

14ᵗʰ January

Singapore Airlines sounds pleasingly exotic. The moment TD read out their menu, her words united immediately and alarmingly with my stomach. My jaw dropped open, saliva ran. The carpet, well… I'm lying on top of it, hoping my body heat will act as a sponge.

Fried carrot cake, Otak-otak and Nasi Lemak – all dishes completely new to me. True, I'm partial to anything carroty but, would the spices suit my delicate stomach? And Moules Frites on Air France could be a problem for my lactose intolerance. Virgin has to be the safer bet and I love the uniform. Virgin Atlantic to a desert island.

I hope they tie a napkin round my neck. A plastic bib with a shelf for catching crumbs cannot be classed as chic. I'm angling for a haircut. This is absolutely, one hundred per cent the right occasion for a poodle cut. If I disguise myself as a *Kennel Club* pedigree, it'll boost our chances of an upgrade.

16th January

I thought I knew all the regulars in Greenwich Park. But today we met Rosie, who owns a dog named Fred who should be called Lassie – he's the hairiest dog I have ever seen. Fred is a park angel and home devil. In the park, Fred is one model dog. At home, he barks at the postman so aggressively, *Royal Mail* is refusing to deliver. Rosie received no cards at Christmas.

Getting rid of Fred was a choice she has not made. Rosie is moving to the country, buying a house with a large garden and a postbox separated from the house, like those on American films. Fred is one expensive dog. I am a home angel and park devil, the cheaper option, TD hopes.

17th January

The West Country is covered in snow. It's coming our way.

18th January. One again, my official birthday!

I raced across the park, through the snow. Soft and fluffy like meringues without the sweetness, but same as a sugar rush. Sends you nuts.

I chased the crows, the dogs I usually avoid and jumped up at a woman wearing a white coat. I wish I could say I didn't spot her in the snow, but that's a lie, I did. I planted two extremely dirty footprints on her chest. I thought they looked like an expensive design, possibly *Longchamp (Paris)*. She didn't see it that way.

Telling her I was overexcited about my birthday tea didn't wash. Offering to clean her coat did. Until that moment I hadn't been on a lead in the park since I was twelve weeks. One year old and I hadn't come up to scratch.

I think two is going to be my perfect age. I may be moving the goalposts, but it's best to be realistic and gives me a little breathing space.

Jacob came round bringing a cake he'd iced. Delish! While the grown-ups stayed in the kitchen drinking wine, we were sent off to watch cartoons. Instead, we caught jelly babies. Having a large mouth helped. Jacob wasn't bad, but

I was better. It's good for him to have something to aspire to. We both agreed we needed more practice.

19th January

'It's a mad world, my masters.' Up in the woods with Jacob for an adrenalin rush not previously witnessed. Families tobogganing, building snowmen the size of polar bears and chucking snowballs at each other, on purpose.

I caught one after another, but, unlike tennis balls, they combust on impact. I quit before my beard froze solid, chased the sledges instead, shooting up hill and down dale trying to keep track of Jacob. An impossible task when all children looked identical. I fancied tobogganing, but hands are better than paws for hanging on and I fell off.

It was patently obvious everyone was having a better time than me. Well, until I stole a piece of carrot cake. Since we live in a blame culture, I'm holding TD responsible. Did I ask to be hooked on carrots and what sensible person leaves a rucksack open? After much grovelling, TD learnt it came from a café, so off she trudged to replace it. I sat in the car, snow tingling on my fur, the taste of carrot cake lingering on my tongue. TD returned empty-handed. I'd eaten their last slice. She coughed up two quid instead.

1st February

TD has finally dragged herself away from her laptop and started packing. We're off tomorrow.

"Dum, dum, dum, de, dum, de, (pause) dum, de, dum, de, dum." Her humming is driving me crazy. TD says Cliff Richard's *Summer Holiday* song is on a loop in her brain. Never heard of him myself. He's not on the radio and who'd call a baby Cliff?

We're getting an early night.

2nd February

On this dark February morning we bundled into the car. The 'we' being rather more than I was expecting: TD, Jacob and family, plus Ivana from next door. No one told me she was coming. Was I supposed to absorb this knowledge like some sort of mental osmosis? And then there was the luggage, a baffling collection of bags. I positioned myself next to Jacob with an excellent view of the road. TD wouldn't need a map with me in the car.

Ivana, who is never easy to understand at the best of times, decided to immerse herself in the lingo: French. Were we heading to Morocco, Mauritius or the colder climes of Europe? A paradise island or a ski slope? Whichever, Ivana spent the entire journey practising on me.

Not wishing to boast, but I am considered a bit of a linguist. Having collected Jacob from after school French club since day one, I know loads of vocab and I'm not talking *Frère Jacques* or *Un, Deux, Trois, Cat Sank*. In fact, with the exception of Jacob, I was liable to be the only one in the car to understand Ivana, my family being utter rubbish at languages.

'*Bonjour, mon petit chien, comment ça va?*' Oh please, we hadn't even got out of our drive. I could see I was going to struggle.

'*J'attend le jour avec impatience.*' How could I concentrate on map-reading with her rabbiting down my ear? If I didn't keep a sharp look-out for the Gatwick turn-off, we'd miss the plane.

Only when the sun came out, did my concentration waver. '*Le soleil est trop chaud. J'ai mal à la tête. J'ai besoin de l'ombre. Puis-je changer de place?*' How would she cope on a desert island? We all got out and swapped places and Ivana was happy until…thirty minutes later we turned east.

'*Le soleil est dans mes yeux.*' And yes, she was back on the sunny side. The car stopped. All change!

'*Pourriez-vous fermer la fenêtre? Il y a un courant d'air.*' Now this was beyond the pale. I lay down for a kip. Big mistake. The next time I stuck my nose out the window, it was too late. TD had taken the wrong turn.

We stopped in a concrete field behind queues of cars. Men in booths checked our tickets and directed us to various lanes. We filled in the time by eating breakfast. Jacob and I demolished an entire packet of custard creams.

'*Voilà, Dougal! Tu ne mange pas mon sandwich. Pas de croque monsieur pour toi,*' said Ivana, waving her breakfast under my nose. '*Fromage est dangereux pour les chiens.*' Well, she got that right. '*Tu pourrais mourir.*' Let's hope not.

The cars in front revved up and our lane moved off. After a passport check we drove on to a train. Would this take us to our plane?

Eurotunnel is a small, narrow box. There is no space, no view. It's boring, but fast. The others got out and stretched their legs, a pleasure denied me. What if I used the train as a *pissoir*? The reek of stale urine confirmed many humans already had. Before I'd time to grumble we were off, driving past warehouses and factories, in a land that was as dull and flat as a pancake. The skies were grey, the landscape greyer, and the cold wind swept right through the car. So much for light at the end of the tunnel.

Eventually, we stopped in the largest car park I'd ever seen, filled to bursting with vehicles, people and carts. They disappeared inside a huge concrete building, leaving me behind to keep an eye on things – which was on a par with watching paint dry. Trolleys, stacked with boxes, were emptied into cars, removed, reloaded and returned, a pattern that repeated itself with monstrous and monotonous repetition. If my family did this, would there be room for me? And yes, they did. And no, there wasn't.

Bottles and boxes, tins and cheeses were packed into the car. Then more bottles, boxes and tins – enough to supply an army. OK, OK, I'm having a whinge. Of course I love going everywhere with TD and have always considered myself a bit of a shopaholic – so good being in touch with one's feminine side. But this had to go down as the worst shopping experience in history.

'*J'ai faim,*' Ivana cried. 'I'll faint if I don't eat.' Food? I brightened up as packages of ham, sausage and cheese were ripped open. When our stomachs were full, we headed for home.

If only it had been that simple. If only TD had done her homework. I should have seen a vet on arrival. We'd have to stay the night. 'Oh, great!' they all cried. 'More retail therapy!'

Summer holidays, eh? Promises, promises. Will my dream ever come true? Cité Europe was never on my wish list, nor is it one of the hundred places to visit before you die.

I was dangerously close to shooting round to Tiger's for a bottle of valium, when TD blocked my exit – oh boy, can that woman read my mind!

'Dougal, don't give me that poor-me look, especially when I've spent a small fortune on our holiday.'

My floppy ears perked.

'Yes, a holiday, in Brittany. I needed practice driving on the right.' Well, you could have knocked me down with a baby squirrel. I pictured the beaches in the brochures: the miles of sand, palm trees and waiters serving cocktails. We'd have to watch out for those German dogs bagging the sun loungers. With my pale complexion, would I require factor 50? And how long had we got to get body-beach-ready? Wait a sec. Where was Brittany? Was it a desert island? Did they speak French? As I fell asleep, Cliff Richard's *Summer Holiday* was on a loop in my brain.

6th February

After all that spend, spend, spend, it had to happen. We're on an economy drive. Christmas, followed by excessive retail shopping, means we're flat broke.

TD has jettisoned her smart Greenwich hairdresser for a shop in an inferior location, smashing the bill from forty quid to seven. The best thing about the *Bridge Lane Barbers* is its position, sandwiched between an off-licence and a burger bar, a spot where kids hang out after school. Now, either rubbish isn't part of the school curriculum or their arms aren't long enough to reach the bins, for wherever children congregate the pavements are littered with edible detritus, perfect for dogs.

Just done a recce. I positioned myself under a huge window smothered in posters of guys with fabulously sculpted hairstyles. People-watching is my number one pastime, now that shopping's dropped off the fun list.

First thing to grab me, not literally, was the sight of an Adonis sprawled on a black shiny sofa, gazing with undisguised pleasure at his reflection in the mirror. A face, crowned in the identical designer hair as the hunks on the posters, stared coolly back. Wow. I took a deep breath and pressed my nose hard up against the glass. Initially, the shop looked void of custom, then, at the very back, through a thick patch of fog, I saw something move. It wasn't a rat.

TD entered and the blast of air she took in with her cleared my vision. Jammed at the back of the shop, in a space no larger than a sock, a tea party was taking place. All thoughts of chicken bones vanished. A row of old girls, two buried under mammoth mushrooms, read magazines and gossiped while a plump lady fussed over them, handing out cake and sympathy.

'You all right, love; that cough better? Same colour as last time?' The jolly woman ran up and down the row, serving, snipping, pinning and chatting.

'Doll, have a biscuit. Go on, force yourself.'

'Don't mind if I do.' The snacks kept on coming, the aroma drifting through the letter box till I was weak at the knees. This had to rank alongside the Queen's Garden Party.

Steam burst through the kettle, rose from the dryers and wafted over the cups. At moments it was hard to see through the mist. Then a bell rang, and it was all systems go.

'Your turn, Lil, and you, Brenda.' As two old biddies emerged from the mushrooms, the next went under. No sooner were their rollers out than the teasing and brushing began. I couldn't believe it. They had tight blonde curls, just like me! Had they asked for a poodle cut? Could I come here?

'In a hurry, Bets? Mind if I do this lady first?' It was TD's turn. What style would she choose? We could be twins, dog and mistress lookalikes.

She was out in a flash: short hair, no curls. No wonder it was cheap. Did she ask about me, did she? Did she book me in?

The cost-cutting includes energy bills…

No ironing – like did she ever?

Fewer baths – let's hope that includes me.

Less heating, extra jumpers on – I hope that doesn't include me.

Lights off. If TD doesn't want me to fall downstairs, break a leg or worse, she'd better increase my carrot rations, pronto.

8ᵗʰ February. 2 p.m.

TD took Jacob to *SeeWoo* and bought him a dragon, giant chopsticks, a mask and a fan. She spends more money on him than me. And I thought we hadn't a pot to piss in.

4 p.m.

Home barely an hour and he's already pulled all the sequins off his dragon. She's wasted her money.

10ᵗʰ February. Year of the Snake

TD and family are off for a meal at the *Peking Duck*. I'd like to sit outside, eating spare ribs and fortune cookies. But I am home, gutted and dying for a doggy bag. While I await the delivery, I'm lounging on the sofa in front of the telly, immersing myself in Chinese culture.

What a learning curve and thrill to discover the Chinese adore animals, particularly dogs. We're revered and, unlike here, preferred to cats. There is no year of the cat – I refuse to count tigers. And if there's no year of the cat, I doubt there are any *Cat Protection* charity shops in Beijing streets. Who said ignorance was bliss?

As I learn more about my sunny nature I discover my body: whichever bit my personality lives in is housing a rabbit as well as a goat. Yes, born in the Year of the Rabbit. From my rabbit personality I receive a long life, kindness, hatred of disagreements and elegance – and I'd assumed it all boiled down to being part poodle. Indy gets his strength, energy and arrogance from his dragon family. Indy's inability to accept treats, without snapping a finger off, suddenly all adds up.

What's more, I find TD is born in the Year of the Dog. Now this speaks volumes.

It's said dogs often believe they're human or that humans are dogs. So, if TD has a dog inside her, it means one twelfth of the world's dogs are owned by a dog or at the very least by an owner who is as much dog as human. Thinking about all this is doing my head in.

I pray there are no further horoscopes with animals needing accommodation. That section of me is full.

14th February
Valentine's Day has come and gone without a card. Have I lost all my friends? Am I unloved? Rosie's day also came and went without a card. Did the postman have one for her that he refused to deliver, or is she, too, unloved?

15th February
I'm seeing stars. They are black with ears. Photos of this 'baby' plaster our walls. A huge one dominates the mantelpiece. When I say huge, I'm talking mammoth, way larger than the actual beast. His eyes follow me wherever I go, his smile nauseatingly smug. The only difference between his picture and the Mona Lisa is, he's got a shoe in his mouth. Hannah's. Indy walks around the house with it. He doesn't chew it; it's what gun dogs do. He's a picker; it's in his genes.

Now, I know my behaviour is out of my control, I'm refusing to listen to all commands.

16th February
It's bitter, cold enough to freeze your nose off. So what does a frog do? Only dumps a load of spawn in a disused plant pot in our garden, a vessel I banked on for additional water.

It's frozen solid. We are calling the lovely Lois for advice. TD says she has an affinity with frogs on account of their annual use of her pond.

Lois believes they will thaw out, like test-tube babies.

17ᵗʰ February

Clever or what! When Hannah and Luke left Indy alone for hours, he didn't tear any wallpaper, chew shoes or wet the floor: he found a toilet. A human toilet – jumped up, balanced and hit the target. Talk about proud parents.

The more I think about it, the more I wonder, can this be true? Is there a photo? Feeling deeply inadequate and have turned to comfort eating – a sock.

18ᵗʰ February

Got wind of this in the grapevine: Ivana has a new boyfriend. He's only a Virgin pilot and does long-haul. This means I'd watch the flight from the captain's cabin.

Sudden thought. Is he aware of Ivana's neurosis or should someone spill the beans? If he turns up wearing black, this could be the briefest relationship. Can we fit a holiday in before it's over?

Terrific news! I might even grow to like the little beast. Indy's one puppy class wasn't sufficient. He's off to Boot Camp for a two-week intensive course. It will cost an arm and a leg.

His word count is increasing. He now knows ten words. This is not something to brag about. At his age I knew hundreds. His grasp of the Queen's English is pathetic. TD says gun dogs react to hand signals, not words. If she's right, what happens in the dark?

19ᵗʰ February. 9 a.m.

This may turn out to be a desperately sad, get-your-hanky-out story. I'm ill. Not a little bit ill, really, really ill, in fact dying. It's no joke. It's not man flu. Can't eat, can't drink, can't walk, can only lie on the sofa.

2 p.m.

Emergency appointment with Alan. Almost a blue-light job. It's sure to be Chronic Active Hepatitis or Bundle Branch Block, probably both.

Had two jabs. One nearly killed me. Got weighed. Another two kilos lost. That's four that have gone missing. If I survive this – and there is some doubt – I'll be on special rations.

Went home with Dioralyte. It was that or go on a drip. I quite fancied staying, but gathered there's no flat-screen TV and I wouldn't be sleeping on Alan's bed. Drugs hadn't kicked in, so vomited all the way home. Daren't go into details. TD is out, cleaning the car. Am allowed sticky rice and chicken. Do they think I'm Chinese?

20th February. 10 a.m.

Have decided NIL BY MOUTH is my best bet. Alan says if I continue along this path, I'll become dehydrated and the drip won't be an option. Walks are off-limits until I'm better. Will I ever be better? The upside is, been allowed to sleep next to TD just like a real person, head on pillow, my body alongside hers. If I play my cards right this could (if I survive) become my permanent place.

1 p.m.

Taken many turns for worse and my friends are desperately worried. Their concern is helping me stay positive. Keep telling myself I have much to live for: family, friends, swimming.

5 p.m.

Going for committal, in a cage, on a drip. Alan believes I have an obstruction, in which case I may need an emergency operation. It'll be touch and go.

22nd February

Forty-eight hours later. Shaken, but thankfully still part of the world, I'm out, weak and five kilos lighter. TD is deeply relieved and £600 poorer. Overjoyed, until she heard the cause of my obstruction: a sock, a very expensive sock. The word 'pea-brain', was voiced again. I can't connect cause and effect. There's a chance, a strong one, I may do it again. I'm desperately hoping I won't.

Against my better judgment, I'm off to Barnes Farmers' Market tomorrow. Let us pray St John Ambulance is standing by. TD argues she can't leave me at home, the trains will be empty and I'll meet the Scottish dog lover, Sharon. Piece of cake. The last three words sold it to me. Sadly, my view of the event didn't quite tally.

PLUS COLUMN
Stopped by artist who wanted to paint me
Scottish dog lover promised to knit me a coat
Ate seven Amaretti biscuits
Trains really were empty
Spotted gorgeous black retriever on Teddington train – must be on the mend

MINUS COLUMN
Absence of St John Ambulance
Tied up to gate of Farmers' Market again
No sausages allowed. Diet imposed by vet
Scottish dog lover only had baby-pink wool
Cocked my leg. Man called me disgusting (full info below)

The Complete and Unabridged Story of my Urination at Waterloo Station
Exact position of incident: the graded walkway between SE and SW overground trains.

Reason for episode, dire emergency, caught short, leg-crossing impossible. As I balanced on three legs, with fourth in perfect arabesque, hot golden liquid gushed forth. Up and up it sprayed, as impressive as an Icelandic geyser. I was in awe, my fellow commuters less so. A man shuddered.

'That's disgusting,' he said. And how did TD reply?

Did she say, 'This poor little dog, that normally holds his bladder for seventeen hours, is only just back from the brink of death?' No!

Or even, 'Excuse me, sir, had you spent forty-eight hours on a drip, wouldn't your bladder have reached saturation point, be stuffed beyond capacity with water and require frequent emptying?' Like hell she did.

So what exactly were her words? 'I quite agree. He's behaving like a drunk on a Saturday night.' Thanks for standing up for me, mate.

3ʳᵈ March

It's been a week of non-stop abuse. OK, so it's verbal, but they say it can turn physical at a whim. I'm watching my back.

Monday. 'I see Dougal hasn't lost his reputation as the dirtiest dog in Greenwich.' I was capsized by this remark. Do they realise the impact of their words? If I had short hair there'd be less of me to collect all this mud.

Tuesday. 'Stick him in the washing machine.'

Wed. 'Looks like a man in a dog suit. If you unzipped him, two clowns would fall out.'

Thurs. 'Oy, shagpile.'

Friday. A man asked if I was a banker's poodle, then laughed hysterically. This was the final straw. And what on earth is that?

Back in the garden, I found the frogs had done it again. Is this the work of one frog, or a joint effort? Their colossal output is staggering and, for a castrated chap, a real kick in the teeth.

Important info: I am still sleeping on the bed and plan to continue.

4ᵗʰ March

I was hungry, tired and fractious. The day didn't bode well.

I knew it, just knew it. My life's goal of becoming a fat dog is a mere pipe dream. TD has her nose buried in books about diet and longevity: The CR Way, On/Off days. In other words, CALORIE RESTRICTION. Even if they're for her, there's bound to be a spin-off – me. Do I want to outlive my friends, receive a card from the Queen or be so emaciated people mistake my ribs for a xylophone? Give me a short, happy, fat-fuelled life.

I'm dreaming of ice-cream, cakes, and Mrs Beeton's feasts: calves' head pie, boiled mutton and stuffed pigs' feet. Why am I not living with Nigella?

5th March

Been out foraging! It's rubbish day, a highlight on my weekly calendar. The Tuesday Special, not exactly a pub menu, provides excellent opportunities for additional food, in a three-tiered operation. Foxes take the first sitting. Once they've finished, we dogs gobble up their rejects – leftovers, amounting to a sizeable calorie count. And when we're replete, the bin men sweep everything away.

I can't help but feeling hard done by when I see the superiority of our neighbours' diets. Hash browns, tinned spaghetti, Chinese chicken wings and give me an Asda's Own Lasagne over one of TD's home-made ones any day.

Results not good: got the runs, back on rice. Weight loss guaranteed. Will I ever be at peace with my body?

8th March

Indy is back from Boot Camp. Hannah and Luke have been severely reprimanded. He is behaving badly because his immense brain is lacking stimulation. If Indy doesn't start gun dog training soon, he'll become depressed and destructive. My heart bleeds for him.

Do I have a purpose? What careers are there for meet and greet dogs like me, unless as a doorman at The Savoy? TD says this is implausible and I need to man-up.

9th March

Crufts: I couldn't be arsed. Despite being nudged in the ribs, incessantly, I slept my way through this TV programme I was supposed to enjoy. The few bits I caught looked utter torture; dogs skipping here, tight turn there, up and down, wrapping round the ring. A tough challenge, I'd say, and penalties for not handling the carpet well. How well can any dog handle a carpet? Only thing I learnt was the poodle in me has a water-repellent coat. Too right! I'm the only dog I know who couldn't give a monkey's about rain.

10th March

Luke and Hannah should get a refund. Indy's been rejected as a gun dog: short-sighted and no sense of smell. Am picking myself off the floor!

He's off to agility classes instead. Agility means jumping. I need to go. TD says she's time-poor. What about my rights? Life's unfair.

11th March

Common sense has prevailed. TD is reading and rereading the diet books. From her hunched back and mutterings, I can tell she's not a fan.

'I don't bloody believe it!' is the least of her expletives. 'Let some other sucker have them.' The books are being returned to *Amazon* and we're chugging along as before, until the next drama occurs.

13th March

My annual health check. How time does fly. After a thorough examination, Alan told me I'm left-handed, a piece of information that thrills TD but leaves me cold, especially as I haven't a clue which is which. Surely ambidextrous would be better? The bad news is my tennis ball fixation has worn down my incisors. If I continue treating tennis balls as chewing gum, I'll need dentures by the time I'm five. Trying to avoid doom and gloom.

14th March

Indy's agility classes are going splendidly well. He is the star pupil. So the cocky little beast has had a brilliant week, unlike me. Got compared to a glove puppet, some star from a bygone era; a dreadful double act that must go down as the most annoying programme in TV history. Sooty's friend, Sweep: a shaggy grey dog with floppy black ears, a squeaky voice and eyes like piss holes in the snow.

Let's get this straight: I don't have black ears, unless caked in mud, and I rarely squeak, so where's the connection? It's got to be the eyes. If only TD would cut my hair I'd never

a) miss my ball,

b) walk into trees and lamp posts,

c) be compared to a glove puppet. They'll be calling me Shaun the Sheep next.

And guess what, they did. I was only sitting outside *Waterstones*, conveniently close to McDonald's, nose to ground, hoovering up chicken bones, gum, fag ends, you name it, when two guys sidled up to me and asked, 'What the hell is a sheep doing here?'

At that moment, I, who according to TD, with the one exception of Christmas have never been nickable – too dirty for Greenwich, not butch enough for Lewisham – feared for my life. I could visualise the atrocities of the abattoir, taste the Dougal-style lamb with mint sauce. Was this to be my destiny? Here I was, not eighteen months old, my life in jeopardy. Before I could raise the alarm, TD appeared swinging a bag of books, confirmed I was a sheep and, without an ounce of sympathy, yanked me away.

16th March

Sometimes invitations come from unexpected places and in this freezing month of March one did. To TD's amazement it came through the post.

I have to admit I was surprised and chuffed to receive an invite from a dog I actively dislike and frequently bite – so very un-me. Shirty Bertie happens to be the most annoying dog in the park prancing about in his *Crufts* poodle cut and nibbling my bottom. But he belongs to three little girls and I'm partial to girls and girls are partial to me. I probably remind them of their teddies.

Dear Dougal
Please come to my party on Easter Monday at 3 p.m.
Do not bring any presents (although a bone or biscuit would be welcome).
Dress code: SMART
Latecomers will not be welcome
Games to start punctually at 3.15
Tea 4.15
Do not eat before you come
Make sure you are collected at 5.30 sharp
Love Bertie (pawmark)
PS Please ensure you poop before arriving
RSVP

Address:
House opposite pond, close to the Princess of Wales pub

TD almost fell off her perch. And there was more.

The Menu
Please tick food preferences

At this, TD gave a short scream and spilt her coffee. She swore it wasn't the after-effects of the night before.

TREATS
Cocktail sausages (GF – Gluten Free)
Oven-baked liver morsels

MAIN TEA
James Wellbeloved honey balls (no good for canines with poor teeth)
Pizzas (bad for all those with weight problems; contain

gluten)

Sainsbury's Taste the Difference Pork Pies (bad for both the above)

Cheddar cubes (contain dairy)

Carrot sticks – GF & DF

Beef crisps – GF&DF

Cat-food sandwiches, cut into heart shapes, topped with sprinkles. (For those dogs denied the pleasure of Felix and Whiskas, you're in for one heck of a treat.)

DESSERT
Good Boy choc drops
Mr Kipling's Apple Pies (contain gluten and dairy)

BEVERAGES
Sweet tea/water/milk – neither dairy nor lactose free
Soya milk – on request

GAMES
100 metres. Long jump. High jump.
Best in show. Best costume (have my eye on this prize).

PRIZES
Balls
Dental sticks
Dog Chocs

GOING HOME BAG
Marrow bones

Who'd been invited? What would we wear? Was it an April fool? Party chatter dominated our walks through the coldest March since records began. Would it live up to Jacob's pirate party, I wondered.

The guest list turned out to be:
JR, Chilli, Archie and Basil (all intact German pointers)
Tiger, terrified of small dogs and loud noises

Titch, neurotic and determined to kill all large dogs

Megan, a large, well behaved labradoodle, the birthday boy and me – nine in all.

20ᵗʰ March

Comments over my appearance continue to flow but make not one jot of difference.

'Dirt magnet!' 'Revolting!' 'Repugnant!' 'Stick him in the washing machine!' Is she deaf, heartless or both?

When TD went out leaving me alone and the bedroom door ajar, I did what any sensible hound would do. I took advantage of the situation. And as I lay sprawled across the pillows, admiring my profile in the wardrobe mirror, I had a revelation. Even if there was only one member and that member was me, I had a fan club.

21ˢᵗ March

She's capitulated. Not because her stone heart has melted, she's had her ears syringed or wants me to win the best-dressed dog prize. It all boils down to our British weather. The driest year on record has turned into the wettest in history. Each morning we leave the house dry and return drenched. TD merely wet; me wet, filthy, caked, coated and stinky. Actually, I honk: require a bath and shower with shampoo and conditioner, followed by a blow dry. In other words: hours of time. It would wear anybody down. It's worn TD down.

Where will she take me: *Scruffs 2 Crufts* or *Dog About Town*? She's bought a pair of electric cutters, a dog version of a hedge trimmer, a money-saving device, no doubt.

22ⁿᵈ March

My coat is so matted the machine has been dropped in favour of scissors. I am having frequent haircuts in the garden. The birds are benefitting. Their nests now have thermal linings, blond.

I'm told it's good to be charitable, but if we get more snow, this could have been over-generous on my part. I may need a coat.

25ᵗʰ March

I dashed to the park with my new stylish cut, excited at the thought of positive feedback.

'What a truly sorry state. What the hell have you done?' Tiger's boss never knowingly minces his words.

'I'm working from the top down,' TD replied.

'What with, the carving knife?'

Does this mean I look ridiculous?

26ᵗʰ March. 5 p.m.

Another grooming session. Due to sub-zero temperatures, an inside job. Result, sitting room carpeted in thick blond hair, hoover broken.

27ᵗʰ March

Back in the park; their reactions showing no signs of improvement.

'My God, is that Dougal? He looks like a patchwork quilt.'

'I'm doing one leg at a time.' Best swap: 'doing' for 'hacking'.

28ᵗʰ March

I have to hand it to her: TD has an answer for everything. I now have a *WORK IN PROGRESS* notice strapped to my back. And that's stopped all remarks, rude or otherwise. The chances are TD wasn't a hairdresser in her last life.

What news of party clothes? There are rumours of a costume. If it's Rudolf, I shall refuse to co-operate.

31ˢᵗ March

Easter Sunday: what a rip off! Chocolate eggs, chocolate bunnies, chocolate chicks, chocolate, chocolate, chocolate – all for them. For me, nothing, thanks to some nonsense theory about chocolate being poisonous for dogs. Honestly, however much I pestered, they refused to share even the tiniest sliver.

Bored witless, stuck in my basket, waiting. Tomorrow is my day.

1ˢᵗ April, bank holiday Monday. 12 p.m.

My personal stylist, just the one, called Jacob, arrived with a choice of clothes for me to try. Now we may weigh roughly the same, but our shapes differ. For a start, he hasn't got a tail. How on earth was I going to fit into a Ninja costume with mask, belt and dagger, or even a smart outfit?

I was no longer a man dressed in a dog suit but a dog dressed in a man suit. I wore a bow tie, shirt and shorts with a hole in the back for my tail. Zip open for peeing access. Could I bag the Best-Dressed prize?

2.30 p.m.

The pavements were packed with families heading to the fair on the Heath. We'd left in oodles of time, but my clothes attracted attention and we got waylaid. People stopped to chat and take photos. Jacob lifted a paw for them to shake, while TD explained. Down the line, meet and greet; what I do best. I felt like royalty, except no flowers were strewn and I wore no gloves. By the time we turned on to the Heath, I knew I was cute, adorable and in need of a personal trainer. Yes, I'm loath to admit this, I'd discovered the power of dressing and the pleasure of fame.

3.10 p.m.

The venue was easy to spot. Balloons tied to gate, Birthday Boy banner over the door. We rushed across the Heath, past the pond and rousing music pumping from the fair to join Megan and the German pointers. Trust them to be punctual. Megan in a red tutu, the others sporting super-smart jackets. No competition so far on the clothing front, but Little and Large had still to appear.

We hung about, polite and awkward, a pack of hounds dressed up like dogs' dinners, waiting for our friends. First Tiger lumbered round the corner in a Superman T-shirt, then hot on his heels came Titch, clothed in such quantities of lacy bows I mistook him for a gypsy bride – a real contender for the Best Dressed Dog prize. But, in his haste to be first over the threshold, he chucked up his entire breakfast, splattering his costume with polka dots of semi-digested biscuit. Titch was home for a shower before he reached the door.

After a moment of calm, the balloons began popping and Tiger, fearing it was Bonfire Night, turned tail and broke into a gallop. Sixty kilos of dog pulling a man who'd joined Slimming World only last week. Neither was prepared to give way, Tiger racing to his bathroom cabinet for rescue remedy; Andy skimming along the pavement on his arthritic knees, filling the air with expletives. We were two dogs down. The party hadn't begun.

Then the front door opened and a host of little girls ran out with the Birthday Boy. Strut your mutt or what? We were wowed, rooted to the spot by this king of eye-popping colour. Shirty Bertie; crimped, pimped and dyed. My confidence bombed.

'Keep your nose clean,' were TD's parting words. The bosses gone, we were on our own. The girls ushered us through a side gate to the back garden, a mini replica of Greenwich Park with pond, tennis court and a row of chairs, oddly placed, between two urns.

Before we could run riot, the party kicked off with Best-In-Show. Not behaviour classes; they had to be kidding. What about Pass the Parcel and Blind Man's Bluff? I lay down and sulked. Call me a party pooper, I didn't care and where was our promised tea? The smells from next door's BBQ were driving me nuts. I had the hump all right.

Then I caught the words, 'MUSICAL CHAIRS'. My ears pricked, as much as floppy ones can. The iPod went on. One Direction sang *Live While You Are Young*, and I joined the party spirit.

We hopped on to our seats, chests puffed, beautifully erect, ready for a game we were utterly clueless about. A line of perfect pets; three to one side, three the other, Megan on the ground in the middle, waiting for a larger chair to be fetched from the kitchen.

This was the mistake. This was the moment when Delia, Delilah and Daphne, three hideous long-haired cats with Bertie-style poodle cuts, strolled into the garden and the party took off. We sat, silently eyeballing each other. Then, in one superbly synchronized leap, the six of us shot off our chairs and the battle commenced. There was a pounding of legs as dogs pursued cats and children chased dogs pursuing cats over tennis net, round lawn and into flower beds. The cats hissed and spat. Why take on six dogs? They were outnumbered. But they were cats, fierce cats, cats with claws.

The garden turned into a battleground. There was no stopping us. Tear gas would have been an acceptable use of force as the stampede continued over grass, through pond, into house and back – an army of dogs moving any child in our path, lifting them up like a huge cloud of dust. The kids were crying, dogs barking, cats yowling. There were dogs in the pond, cats in the pond, draped in more duckweed than I'd achieved in any of my Titchmarsh days. Wet-furred and shivering, they fled up a tree. Six angry eyes bore down on us.

'We'll call the Fire Brigade!' cried the parents as they rushed to the scene.

'You're ruining our bank holiday!' screamed the neighbour from next door.

Suddenly the fun fell out of the day. It was game over; time for the reckoning and the horrifying catalogue of damage to be dealt with. What had I done? I was mortified. I hate to see children cry. Before the *London Fire Brigade* appeared with their ladders and fury at being called out on a bank holiday Monday to rescue three vile cats from the top of a monkey puzzle tree, I left, scaling the wall in one. Dispirited, I wandered off, intending to go home.

It was a combination of things that drew me to the fair: food and the sound of children's laughter, so delightful after the scene I'd left, and why hurry home to face the music? I crossed the road and entered a new, magical world, exploding with energy and excitement. Machines twisting and whirling, spitting out lights and noise at such deafening amplification I feared my eardrums would split. Scary. Intoxicating. Fun.

I put my left foot forward and headed for the burger stalls, my hips rocking gently to a waltz.

I didn't plan to be caught in a revolving teacup, never planned to ride on one. But I'd forgotten my attire: the sodden shorts, the ripped shirt and battered bow tie. As I sauntered through the bustling fairground, I collected children, I was patted, handed hotdogs, candyfloss and popcorn. I perked up. Perhaps I wasn't so bad, after all.

And that's how it happened. How I came to be seated on a revolving teacup, sharing a toffee apple with two small girls, whose parents believed I was lost. When a man in smart uniform approached, I mistook him for an airline pilot. If only I hadn't. When I followed him to his car, I assumed he'd drive me home. He didn't. Instead, we arrived in Lewisham, at a concrete building filled with other identically-dressed men. He found the phone number on my collar, hidden beneath my bow tie. TD was called. I sat in a chair in reception, awaiting collection. I was in the dog house, no kidding.

TD says I could have been stolen, used as bait in dog fights; that I must grow up and learn to take responsibility. Megan had been the only dog at the party to behave. I need to model myself on her.

As a result of today's misdemeanour, I have made an oath. In future I will never join a gang, even against cats. Cats are animals, too. They may have nine lives, but it's not up to me to prove it. On a lighter note, it's imperative Jacob teaches me high five and TD buys me a pair of gloves. I must be ready for my next Royal Occasion.

A quick thought. If curiosity killed the cat, who or what killed the dog? Oh no! How could I forget? The flashing lights could have increased my chances of epilepsy. Was this temporary amnesia my very first seizure?

3ʳᵈ April

Hannah and Luke are no longer an item. Indy might have to stay with us.

How will Ivana cope with a black dog living next door? Should we get Jacob round to paint white spots on him? If he looks like a Dalmatian, she's bound to feel at home.

4ᵗʰ April

I hope TD has read up on the Dangerous Dogs Act. The media is bursting with stories of savaged grannies and mauled children. During the break-up, Indy may have witnessed arguments and irrational behaviour. He could turn violent. We've already had six dead dogs in our park and many whose lives have been saved through the dexterity of Alan. We could be in mortal danger.

5ᵗʰ April

The monster is now living with us. In TEMPORARY ACCOMMODATION ONLY!

Indy is huge, five months old and almost my height. And all thanks to Ambrosia: the elixir of life, food of the gods and creamy rice pudding. How many cans has he actually consumed? Is the proof in the pudding, or in the weight gain?

After four hours, twenty-five minutes and thirteen seconds, my social life is right down the pan. Indy is not a people person and hates children. Visits to Uncle John are out, so is baby-sitting Jacob. Indy only loves Hannah. If she were a kangaroo, he'd be her joey – what a thought.

I hope TD doesn't take up this fostering lark as a full-time occupation. I am hers. She is mine. I do not want to become a mini-Battersea. On the plus side, Indy looks sad rather than aggressive.

6ᵗʰ April

I'm told Indy is traumatised and I should be sympathetic. Damn Indy, I am traumatized. His basket is larger than mine, food portions twice the size and he's invading my space. He even shares TD's bed at night. It's barely a double. We need a queen or king, preferably a replica of *The Great Bed of Ware* on display at the V&A, sleeping twelve. They sure knew how to make a dog happy in the 16th Century.

Despite a carpet of black hairs coating the duvet, sheets and pillows, Indy now takes pride of place next to TD. If this regime continues I shall be forced to sleep on the pillows or move. How many corgis does the Queen have on her four-poster and is there room for another? TD has fallen out of bed on more than one occasion. Action is needed.

TD is dropping Mr Dyson a line, asking him to design a vacuum cleaner for shedding dogs – not the move I was hoping for. In writing this letter she is dodging the issue. TD says Mr Dyson is looking for a project to push his ingenuity to new heights. This top of the range dog vacuum would suck out all the loose hairs and come with a silencer and massaging gadget. *Vorsprung durch Technik.*

Sorry, I consider TD's handling of this affair to be a 'car crash'.

7th April

My bony back has become the homeopathic equivalent of a packet of Kwells.

We travel to the park inside a motorised snail; it's our new morning routine. If the other drivers find our one mile an hour speed infuriating, that's too darn bad. TD isn't keen on dog vomit sloshing around the car. I stand in the boot, Indy at my side with his head resting on my back. A position that soothes his stomach but is hard to maintain when going round corners, or braking sharply, even at a slow speed. By the time we arrive, I'm drenched in slobber.

'Gross,' said Jacob. I agree.

If the puppy continues to eat my food, I shall fade away.

8th April

Indy is refusing to greet my friends, animal or human. The moment we set foot in the park, up shoot his hackles, on 'biting' alert. Indy is terrified of terriers, the kind of fear that makes you want to poop yourself, so he must get in first before they kill him. We are giving Carol and Titch a wide berth.

Whatever led me to think I'd like the little beast? Not only is my social life in tatters, but he's bagged my basket and is gathering a fan club. 'What a beauty!' 'Oh! That's a fine specimen.' These remarks aren't helping me deal with this sudden and undesired change in life.

9th April
Ivana says Indy's blackness is fine by her. She will cope. Shame, Jacob was looking forward to turning him into a Dalmatian.

It has finally been recognised: Indy is greedy and has been put on a diet. First step in the right direction.

15th April
The neighbours are refusing to talk to us. We may have to move. Indy is barking so loudly, no one can sleep. He's out in our garden, chasing foxes both real and imagined, a day and night-time activity. And thanks to Jacob, who crawled round the kitchen testing the kit, the anti-bark collar is kaput, we're out of batteries and citronella spray. The garden is wrecked and TD going bananas. Joy, oh joy!

17th April
Indy only sat through the whole of BBC2's *Queen Victoria's Children* (no balls, food or animals in sight) followed by *The Art of Venice, old and new*. He could be an academic or a journalist, either way MENSA material. Indy lives on nerves and rescue remedy, me, on small portions of food and hope.

20th April
Best news: Hannah is looking for a flat that allows dogs. They will be reunited soon. How soon is soon? Meanwhile, I remain bottom of the pecking order. I'm sure the lack of

attention I receive is bordering on neglect, yet only this morning someone called me the jolliest dog in the park. How come I remain so cheerful?

Indy may be more agile than me, cleverer, more beautiful and funnier, but is he as happy as me? Being gifted comes at a price: he's insecure, depressed and requires a dummy. Instead, Indy has a blanket he sucks like a toddler, only his is black and covered in pawmarks. He greets TD with it, parades it round the house and garden, if mislaid, uses whatever's at hand. His duvet has been dragged through the hall, out the front door and along the pavement. Underwear, a leaf, even five-pound notes have made this same trip. TD finds this hugely amusing. I'm sure if I did it she wouldn't laugh.

25th April

At last we've found some common ground: our stomachs. Indy loves my taste in food: cabbage, carrots, cake. But despite his greed, he refuses to eat celery, proving Joe Debono right. TD worked with this Maltese chef, a good Catholic and vegetarian who hated celery with a vengeance. Joe believed celery was created on God's day off. Only the one, else who knows what else we'd be forced to eat.

Celery is just about the only vegetable that takes so long to chew and digest, you actually lose weight while eating it. It's God's revenge on greedy dogs.

26th April

Indy's hairs are driving TD bats. There's not one second in a 24-hour cycle that dog doesn't moult. By my reckoning, he should have been bald as an egg weeks ago. Hannah has told her to get a new hoover or hire a cleaner. TD has not listened. I think she prefers to complain. When it comes to listening, neither has Indy. He continues to bite the hand offering treats. The dragon inside him remains untrained.

5th May

The Greenwich Park website stipulates no dogs allowed in

the boating pond. But as TD says, few dogs browse the internet so we're carrying on regardless. We stand at the top of One Tree Hill, then in silent agreement are gone, dashing down the slopes, over the grass, past the swings (another forbidden area) and into the pond. Breaking the law adds to the fun.

Finally understood, the power of two is more than double the power of one – I'd never have dared do this alone. Tomorrow, we'll chance it again.

6th May

Am trying to interest Indy in balls, but his real passion is sticks. He's devised a system all by himself, no training, no nothing. He selects one carefully, as I might choose a chew in *Pets at Home*. Next he studies it, cutting it into three identical lengths with machine-like precision. Oh, those muscles! That sheer black strength! I watch, the hopeless creature that I am, admiring his skill and generosity as he hands me the first piece.

Indy may be a smarty-pants, but at least he's not up himself.

7th May

Indy is slowly acquiring my love for balls, so now I'm forced to run twice as fast to get there first. And he drops the ball at TD's feet every time. I think TD is beginning to love him more than me.

9th May

I'm so laid back I'm practically horizontal.

Horizontal is my preferred position, especially with two pillows and a rug draped over my toes. Chillaxing sounds just my style. If it's good enough for Cameron and Boris, it'll be perfect for me.

20th May

After ten whole days in kennels doing absolutely nothing, we got home late last night. The reason for this unthrilling sojourn was TD had a job and the kitchen needed to be dog hair-free days before she started cooking. That woman can kill a dish at twenty yards without the help of Indy's hairs. Since he couldn't have coped in kennels alone, I accompanied him. Kennels are way cheaper than a dog minder but their comfort levels are pitiful. We stayed in a cage with a short covered run. Of the promised fifteen minutes a day exercise, I have no recollection.

We arrived with our bedding, Indy's blanket, a stuffed pheasant (partially chewed) and two tennis balls. Indy's bedding and blanket, dragged up and down the run, had as much exercise as he. We left kennels fat, friends and hyper.

This morning major breakthrough in park: Indy said hello to Tiger.

21st May

Indy has begun nibbling my ears. First one side, then he walks round the back of me to reach the other. Why he goes the long way round, I've no idea. Nevertheless, I find our daily grooming sessions in the boudoir quite delightful. TD considers them extremely smelly and has ordered a case of Stink Bomb from *Pets at Home*.

Indy has been unable to shift his 'kennel week' weight. My cadaverous frame returned in a day.

22nd May

I have started nibbling Indy's ears and giving TD my ball, sometimes. The frogspawn has begun to thaw. TD has put a cake rack over it in case we feel peckish.

24th May

Today the heavens opened and flooding of biblical proportions has turned the roads into swollen rivers. Pavements are a no-go area or take your life in your paws if you dare, as cars with zero visibility swim along streets, creating tsunami-sized waves, which are, I gather, an act of God. All the pets are staying indoors in case our insurance companies refuse to cough up. I am surprised no one, not even Tiger's uncle, who is a carpenter, has built an ark. Does anyone learn from history?

29th May

Our tadpoles have grown legs and can jump for England. I was looking forward to our garden becoming a centre for amphibians. But they're going. Once again, fun snatched away.

TD and Jacob are busy transferring the froglets from basin to buckets, ready for the off. They will travel to Keston Ponds, near Bromley, without us. The drive will be slow. Jacob has made a sign to encourage other vehicles to show respect.

TADPOLES ON BOARD
Pull back
GIVE MY FROGS A CHANCE

Frogs are privileged creatures. I have not seen any PUPPY ON BOARD signs.

30th May

We're slobbing out in front of the television. Indy is a *Mastermind*, *Eggheads* kind of chap, whereas me, I'm your daytime soap kind of guy.

Newsnight has become Indy's favourite programme. He's covering the Syrian disaster in microscopic detail. He must be a member of the Dimbleby Dynasty.

I lie, watching him watching; the chiselled cheek bones, the softest supple lips and teeth so white he could be used on a Colgate ad. When *Newsnight* is over, he picks up his blanket and prances round the room like a dressage stallion, inviting me to play. We wrestle and growl, nibble and nip. The chairs tip over, rugs shoot across the floor and TD yells, 'Stop it! In your baskets, now! You noisy beasts!'

Oh, the ups and downs of life! We're now joined at the hip. It's official.

31ˢᵗ May

Is there such a thing as dogslaughter ? Or is attempted murder, murder? When Indy was attacked by a long-haired vizsla that did it. My brain snapped. The wolf inside me burst forth, baring its teeth and snarling viciously. No one, but no one was going to hurt my little boy. The very next dog I saw, I attacked. Wham, bam, a four-legged battering-ram, in for the kill!

What about mitigating circumstances? There weren't any. The dog I assaulted was totally innocent. He's suffered a severe blow, something similar to whiplash, and is in a state of shock. I too, am in a state of shock. Have I overnight, turned into a pack animal or, worse still, become an aggressive dog and a danger to society?

1ˢᵗ June

Indy is leaving this Friday. Hannah has found a flat in Barnes, near the pond, river and common. Most people in Barnes have black Labs which should help him adjust.

I'm curled up tight as a woodlouse in my basket, hoping it won't happen. I shall be lost without him, bereft. It's called 'empty nest syndrome'. Hannah and TD are worried how we'll cope. Sleepovers and playdates are being hurriedly planned.

8ᵗʰ June

Indy is back with his beloved Hannah. Jacob, TD and I all miss the LB. Jacob said we should mark Indy's absence with a minute's silence – even turned off CBeebies. I'm not sure he can tell the time; it was an extremely long minute.

There are benefits to being the only dog: baby-sitting, seeing Uncle John and having the whole bed to myself. Needed reminding – I'm sharing it with her.

Indy is giving Hannah a hard time, sulking and, oh boy, can that dog sulk. It's having the desired result. Hannah is racked with guilt.

TD is grumbling: she has no more room than when Indy was here. What's the woman on about? She's no less space.

Forced to compromise. Have moved to bottom of bed. If I edge up slowly, she's unlikely to notice.

10ᵗʰ June

Indy was barely back in Barnes thirty-six hours before Hannah was approached. Would she allow Indy to model for the 2014 Labrador calendar? As their cover boy, John Lewis was bound to snap him up and use his face on their new range of tableware. He might even star in their TV Xmas ad.

Hannah didn't need to be bullied into submission. She says it will pay for his keep and anyway it's nothing like being a page three girl. Let's hope she's right. That boy of mine is such a beauty, I always knew he'd be picked up by a talent scout.

11ᵗʰ June

I'm turning into a right ball snob. *Slazenger* versus *Pets at Home* own – there's no comparison. You get a better throw, they're longer lasting and I enjoy being up there with the top professional players: *Slazenger* Wimbledon tennis balls pushing me to the very pinnacle of my prowess. I wouldn't dream of buying them. I hang around the courts in the park and when no one's looking, nick 'em.

13ᵗʰ June

It was a bit of a blunder, but isn't a bag of pastries left on the grass asking to be eaten?

When Paul came round to fix the garden, I ate his carrot cake and two hot cross buns. Had there been three, I'd have eaten three. Paul said, no problem, TD said it was, and gave him an extra fiver. If I'd had pocket money she'd have stopped it for a month.

I need to wean myself off all sugary substances. It's going to be hard, probably worse than quitting smoking and you don't get patches or electric sweets to suck.

15th June

No playdates fixed; the calendar is bare. Out of sight, out of mind. Indy no longer cares about the likes of me – he's too busy having portrait sittings.

Indy's picture is being entered for the Royal Academy's 2014 Summer Exhibition. They'll be queuing round the block.

16th June

I'm not watching the news again; it's too full of awful stories. Today, three large dogs savaged a granny. If I don't stop growing I'll be put down.

Oh Dougal, you are a melancholy soul.

18th June

There has been a proclamation, not from the Prime Minister or Pope, but the procrastinating aunt. Annette is vacating London for the month of October – away with her Morris-dancing team to Australia. Thomas Cook has promised cool weather. I hope they've checked the forecast and let's all pray Annette does not change her mind; we've a whole fifteen weeks to get through. If Thomas Cook doesn't know their customer by now, I wager they will before the month is out.

20th June

Two weeks of the goggle box. Two fun weeks of guiltless couch-potato life.

Excitement grows as Wimbledon looms. But without old Mrs King, it just won't be the same. The fact is: it's going to be a major anti-climax.

22nd June

Dog Trust Fun Day in Greenwich Park
Dog shows
Raw Food Stall
Agility classes,

Designer collars
Get your dog chipped for free
Antler chews
Pick up a box of poo bags
Tennis balls, buy one get one half price.
Battersea Dogs' Home Stall

The Best of Days

A fabulous run. Complete metamorphosis – looking great gives one such a buzz. I was plastered from head to toe in gorse, goose grass and old man's beard. The burrs stuck across my face completed my latest style – might call it the Vivienne Westwood. It deserves a special name. TD said I looked as if I'd suffered a traffic accident and needed plastic surgery. She would.

We had a butcher's at the stalls. A total waste of space as far as I was concerned, the collars too glitzy, the tennis balls rubbish and, as for the antlers, doubtless part of the slow food movement – zero taste and the months of chewing gives you jaw ache. I mooched over to the Battersea booth and dropped my ball, hoping some mug would throw it.

'Hello, you mutt.' It seemed rude to point out I'm an extremely expensive crossbreed, so I sat down like the well-behaved dog I'm not. 'You're exactly the type of dog we're after.' No kidding. I tried hard not to scratch, but some multi-legged insect was crawling through my hair. 'We're looking for a new face for Battersea and you would be perfect.' Perfect? I love that word and wagged my tail encouragingly.

'They only want you because you're a scuffpot.' Oh, not another put-down and how come she always thinks she's right? It didn't bother me she was clearly wrong and high time my design flair received the recognition it deserved.

24th June

Wimbledon has started. No tea is being made, the sofa is empty and the TV is off.

25th June

TD's been forced to take my weight or rather, lack of, seriously.

'Oh no, poor Dougal, is he ok?' 'So, so skinny!' 'So emaciated!' 'Not terminal, is it?' These comments from my friends propelled us to the vet.

What is the diagnosis? What is the treatment? A drip, increased food portions – I was dying to find out.

After a thorough physical examination, Alan declared me entirely to blame for my scrawny body. My inexhaustible energy with balls is the equivalent of a three-hour spin class. No amount of calories can offset all this physical exertion. On the plus side, being thin should guarantee a long life – excellent news, as I'd hate to leave TD. Telling her this and that I have a six-pack has cost a staggering £23.

28th June

My playdate with Indy has been arranged for July 8th. She shouldn't have told me. I'm jumping about like an idiot. I assumed today was the 8th.

30th June
The Worst of Days

I catapulted out of my basket and stood beside TD. It was Battersea on the dog and bone, calling to say they can't use me. It's their policy to employ deserted dogs only.

TD took one look at my hangdog expression and hurried to the freezer for a tub of ice-cream. Two scoops later, I was fast asleep.

5th July

Tea is being consumed. The television is on and Murray is through to the finals. It's a triumph, a British triumph. We're hugging. We're dancing. We are going ballistic. And Mrs King is in the loop; she caught it on the iPlayer. Come Sunday we're skyping: watching it together, us in London, her and son Martin in Spain.

7th July

We were all set for the match. Four souls waiting for tennis fever to begin. Two of us on the sofa, TV tuned to BBC1, computer booted up, ready to skype. And somewhere across the water, Mrs King and Martin sit staring at a laptop, the old girl dressed in her royal-blue best.

Was it the cheering crowds, recognising my hero David Cameron or hearing Mrs King's voice that did it? Who knows, but the result was one thrilled, energy-ridden dog. I tore round the room, bounded over the sofa, clearing it by a fraction, just as a tennis ball might skim the net in an ace serve. Then, as I scooted back on two right legs, like a top-seeded player desperate to catch a drop shot, I almost collided with the TV.

'Dougal,' screamed TD, 'watch out! You'll break the telly.' But I couldn't stop jumping and wouldn't stop barking.

'We can't hear,' complained Spain.

'I can't hear,' shouted London.

'Go on, Murray, get it! Hit it! Oh no! Oh yes!' cried my old friend, grabbing her inhaler. Fans screamed. TD yelled. The crowd erupted. David Cameron jumped up and down in his seat. Could Prime Minister's Question Time ever beat this for noise and excitement? What's the score, I wondered.

'He's fallen to his knees. Get the paramedics!'

'No, Mum, he's fine. He's done it because he's won.'

'Won? He's won? That's my man. I have to join him. I'm getting to my knees.'

'No, Mum, no!' Martin's voice was barely audible over the roaring crowds.

'Well, help me to my feet.' Mrs King got up, saluted, parted her lips and… '*Rule Britannia, Britannia rule the waves.*' Between wheezes and puffs on the vital inhaler, the breathy notes rang out.

'Mum, he's Scottish. Why not, *God Save…*'

'I'm coming to that…' cried the old girl, a royalist to the last. Where did she get her energy from? I was totally done in and gagging for a drink.

In both countries kettles went on. Even in Spain a good English cuppa goes down a treat.

And I thought today's finals wouldn't be a patch on last year!

8th July

Bucolic bliss, the longed for playdate at Stephen's farm had finally arrived.

After weeks of careful planning with only our pleasure in mind, we drove across town to collect Hannah and Indy, before venturing out west. A new route to rack up and add to the ordinance survey map in my head, followed by a country run with pub-stop to eat, meet and greet, or both. And to end the joyous day, a slow drive home in rush hour, allowing plenty of time for collapse and sleep.

Did I notice the views, the hayfields, the sheep, cows or polo ponies, take one look at my friend Indy, even bother to eat horse shit? Not one little bit. I spent the whole time, well, the entire walk on top of a brown gun dog, my paws tightly gripped round his neck, humping. But, what I wanted to shout in my defence was, his name is CHESTER. And considering I'm castrated, it was a triumph.

Hannah and Stephen's laughter made a mockery of my passion. TD kept her eyes averted.

15th July

It's the summer holidays, it's hot and Indy is back for a sleepover. A run in Foots Cray Meadows was on the agenda.

We stopped in the stables car park, shot across the small road with no thought of the green cross code and hit the countryside with wild enthusiasm.

Indy stole food from picnickers, chased all manner of fowl, including a mallard duck he was loathe to surrender – thank god for his gun dog rejection. He was on the lead before the swans swam round the corner.

I raced over the plains and through the streams, then joined TD and Indy under a tree, picking berries – free food begging to be eaten. I gorged myself silly. We were about to leave when I noticed one of my legs drenched in blood. Panic-stricken, I started to limp. By the time we'd reached the car park I could barely walk.

'Don't be ridiculous, Dougal. For God's sake, grow up!' were not the words I wanted to hear. The pain was torturous. Had I torn my dew claw or, worse still, sliced through my post-tibial artery? While TD fumbled for her key I sat beside the car, my paw held high, gasping for sympathy. I knew it looked dramatic, as if I'd stuck my leg in a pot of red paint.

'Oh no, what has your poor dog done?' asked a woman in the car parked beside us.

'Honestly, it's nothing.' You soon know who your friends are.

'Can we help you get him into the car?'

'Thank you, but he's perfectly all right.' Perfectly all right! You sure do know who your friends are.

A dispirited bunch bundled into the car. The radio went on and my leg throbbed to the beat. If it was a main artery, would I live another minute? I pictured a growing pool of blood. Was I suffering from Acute Haemolytic Anaemia? What was my platelet count? And did anyone care? I looked back to my throbbing leg. I needed stitches, antibiotics and a tetanus jab. Would I bleed to death before I reached A&E?

I was given a cold bath and the blood temporarily disappeared. So far, so good, but would it return? Since no medical intervention appeared, it seemed sensible to self-medicate. I began licking the wound. The more I licked, the sorer it became. The sorer it got, the more annoyed TD became.

In her desperation, TD rang the oracle, 'Uncle John, Dougal's driving me nuts. We were out in the country, eating mulberries. You know how badly that juice stains? Well, the darn dog believes it's blood and insists on licking his leg. He's going to do himself an injury if he carries on like this.'

'The silly sausage: get him a crepe bandage and a tube of Savlon.' What? I was reprieved! The hand of death was not about to strike. I charged up and down the hall like an express train, then flopped into my basket, tore off the bandage and proceeded to lick it. Savlon tastes almost as good as clotted cream.

18th July

TD has unearthed the lampshade she'd kept from my castration op. So I now have that to contend with. I'm not a happy bunny.

19th July

Still wearing the dreaded appliance, we drove Indy back to Hannah's. One final run along towpath, headgear removed, leg on the mend. Life looking up, when lo and behold, Indy stole my thunder. He has two cuts across his head and three parallel gashes on his front right leg. Nothing too dramatic, no blood, but limping badly. Is he milking it?

22nd July

No, he isn't. Unable to walk: emergency appointment. Infection has spread to the bone. He's on the critical list. Have I ever been critical?

Indy has been given a proper bandage – looks like a fancy sock – and three injections. I believe one was morphine. He may need an operation, might lose a leg. Running on three can't be easy. Will he need a prosthetic limb?

23rd July

Pus spewing from the wound, operation averted.

We Do Not Like The Cone Of Shame. Indy and I are both kitted out in collars and can be viewed in Hannah's kitchen. We are dipping in and out of depression. At least we have each other.

Indy now has so many scars, his career as a photographic model hangs in the balance. Hannah will not let this happen. She has bought a marker pen, black, naturally, and is filling in the scar lines. I have to admit he looks darn good.

We popped into the garden for a pee in the rain, then hurried back in, keen to dry ourselves on the bedroom floor. Black dye stains have ruined the carpet.

Hannah is out buying a permanent marker pen. This will fix it – Indy's scars, not the carpet.

26th July

'Serendipity!' exclaimed TD when we bumped into Rosie and learnt of the miracles of Mr Heinz. If your dog rolls in fox poo, ketchup camouflages the smell.

Now, is ketchup applied after the dog's been washed or smeared on top of the offending excreta then licked off by the dog? Is Heinz more effective than cheaper brands and who had the nous to try it first?

Although TD says the park is better for information than Google, we did not get the full story. As a journalist who's used to ferreting out the truth, could Rosie please broach the subject next time she chats to Jenni Murray or sits beside a member of the hunt on *Question Time*? Otherwise, the dog-owning population, already weighed down with balls, poo bags, water, treats, mobile phones and keys, will add a superfluous bottle of ketchup to their bulging pockets.

27th July

'Bring a bottle. Bring six. Bring a chair. Bring a stack – and what about nibbles?' It was Hannah's House-Warming Party, an on-the-cheap, do-it-yourself-affair. Hordes of people, two large dogs, one small garden, buckets of rosé wine, pack upon pack of cheese, and enough crisps to open a stall.

Believing we needed a walk before the party, Hannah took us for a run along the towpath. After weeks of rain and high summer tides, it was an absolute bog. If that was bad, the decaying carcass was a thousand times worse. Not for us. We rolled and rolled. No pig, hippo or rhino could have enjoyed themselves more. The stink so rank, we almost passed out.

We were hosed down with, yes, Fairy Liquid, which

produced a mass of bubbles but failed to quell the stench. Talk about in one ear, out the other. What happened to the miracles of ketchup? Hannah ran to the ironmonger and returned with a can of Jeyes Fluid, which she poured over us. Her garden faces south, the sun eventually came out and I dried up. As for the smell, well… Hannah said it was lucky any of the guests stayed.

Indy slunk off to his basket and sulked. He hates sharing Hannah. I had a whale of a time, meeting everyone and dancing with her friends, on two legs just like a real person. And I behaved, I actually behaved. I always knew I was a party animal at heart.

28th July

TD tells me she's a dog's body. Is she finally connecting with her inner dog? Actually, she's joined the Am Drams, the Greenwich Players, and is working behind the scenes, on props and scenery. Let's hope she's not in charge of costumes, her scissor techniques being what they are. Their production of Shakespeare's *A Midsummer Night's Dream* is being performed in the Park. If there's a part for hounds, I might get auditioned. They need an ass for this show.

Will she talk to me in iambic pentameters and rhyming couplets and if she does, will I have a clue what she's on about? It's hard understanding her at the best of times.

30th July

That boy comes up with some stupendous ideas. Jacob was round and TD busy, hence forced to amuse ourselves. What better than a taste the difference cheese-tasting competition? The rivals were Cathedral City and Pilgrims Choice.

Jacob said we preferred Cathedral City, because it's made by bishops who do lots of sitting around rather than by poor folk who have walked too many miles to care about quality. His school studies interesting topics.

To be honest, I hadn't the foggiest which was which. To me, cheese is cheese. I would make a hopeless food judge.

Suffering slight queasiness from dairy overload.

1ˢᵗ August

Snippets from the Bard are coming my way. My favourite so far is:

Jack shall have Jill
Naught shall go ill
The man shall have his mare again
And all shall be well.

A rhyme I whisper to myself when feeling low, except I change the third line.

2ⁿᵈ August

Vanity, thy name is Dougal. My hair has reached the perfect length. I am attractive, cuddly, curly and compliments flow. What a turn-up for the books.

'Nice hair, Dougal.'

'Good Heavens, look at those eyelashes!' A remark that prompted TD to rush home and measure them. I don't wish to sound vain, but they are a staggering 6 cm long, almost 2 ½ inches in old money. I'm sure Lady Gaga's false ones are shorter than mine.

Slight problem: length of fringe depriving me of 20:20 vision.

News Flash: Hannah and TD have decided to flee the capital at Christmas. Indy and I will be staying in the outdoor kennel on Stephen's farm in Oxford. Doesn't sound like a present or party hat occasion; even thoughts of Chester hold no excitement.

So much for spoiling at Christmas.

3ʳᵈ August

What's the matter with me? Life's not exactly a creeping tragedy, but something's up. I'm not my chipper self at all – too young for a mid-life crisis, even a quarter-life one. Mustn't let on, can't worry TD. The last thing she needs is a depressed dog. Expect I'll snap out of it, probably a passing phase. Paws crossed – must avoid the valium.

4th August

A Midsummer Night's Dream went down a bomb. TD returned home, applause still ringing in her ears. Their next production is fixed for the end of September, in the Blackheath Concert Hall – that is one big venue.

5th August

I'm a stickler for exactitude when it comes to meal times. And, TD knows only too well, feeding me after 6 p.m. plays havoc with my body clock. So when she walked in after 7 p.m. – a whole sixty minutes late – I threw her my best hangdog look.

'Don't give me that,' she said. 'It's Ramadan. Thank your lucky stars you're not Muslim.' Who'd be a dog? It's a question I constantly ask.

7th August

Annette has the wobbles. She's been hogging the line for hours. Since I'd been fed, walked and watered, I couldn't moan – hadn't a leg to stand on.

Her friend, Terry, has returned from Auckland a damaged man. When, after a four-hour delay at Heathrow, sitting on a cramped plane it finally took off, the passengers sighed with relief. Two heart attacks, 'Is there a doctor on board?' later, the plane was diverted to the nearest hospital, Kiev.

Terry, who'd left on the Friday a young and happy man after a series of disastrous delays and missed transfers, arrived on the Tuesday, feeling far more than four days older.

Annette has panicked and cancelled her trip – well, I got that right. Says she cannot afford a heart attack or to age unnecessarily. Instead, she is throwing a party for the thirty people she'd asked to look after Kiki for the month she was to be away. Further proof, if proof is needed, that Annette is incapable of making up her mind. Kiki is her cat. Kiki is not nice. She is so not nice no dog would want to chase her.

Remembering her aunt's idea of a brilliant picnic, TD has offered to help. Annette wants it to be an historic occasion.

If her menu containing chicken liver and crème de menthe pâté is anything to go by, I believe it will. My delicate bowels are groaning already. TD is going to have her work cut out.

14ᵗʰ August

I spent the entire week being pushed from pillar to post – we're talking stress here.

I'm worried about life generally, but above all Uncle John and the Homeless. I'll start with Uncle John, who is sick, very sick, in a large London hospital. He's told TD he is not going to live with Jesus, so will pull through – no quick job. His great age is slowing his progress.

As with private hospitals, the NHS has a no dog rule. I can't even be tied up at the desk or left with the staff nurse. OK, I'm not next of kin, but Uncle John and I do have a special relationship. As a result of their shortsightedness I've had to go to my minder or over to Hannah's, spending hours enduring London transport. Over this, my mate Boris has not come up trumps.

Goodness, I'm wandering. The point I'm trying to make is, during all this travelling across our great city, I saw many homeless people, all with dogs, Staffordshire bull terriers – the lost living with the lost. And the dogs looked happy. What I want to know is how they found their owners.

Does a homeless person go to Battersea and say, 'I need a hot-water bottle and a friend,' or someone appear with hundreds of dogs on leads, handing them out like balloons at McDonald's to whoever wants one? And do these dogs get walked by their owners or have a similar set-up to the high flyers at Canary Wharf when on the stroke of noon a man comes round collecting the dogs – in this case, from the Strand or under Waterloo Bridge, and trots them off to a nearby park? Whatever they do works, for I have never seen so many well-behaved dogs in all my life.

TD says Uncle John is not out of the woods. When she told me this, I was in a right old state. Why was he in them? Had he broken out of hospital or lost his mind? Was there a police hunt on?

I needn't have stressed. It's an expression. Uncle John is better, but still unwell. English is a mightily confusing language.

16th August

We're going our separate ways, TD to Bristol and me to Barnes, where Hannah has acquired a lodger. Hannah has given Jacks a bed while she sorts out her life and saves for an Indian trip, a kind gesture that's backfired. Jacks has the TV on all day and shouts down the phone from dawn to dusk, which, as a late riser, means noon onwards. Hannah is spending a small fortune at Costa Café, seeking peace and tranquility.

Indy loathes Jacks with a vengeance. If he could stick pins in an effigy of her and make her ill, I'm sure he would. Instead, he sulks. He also hates his dog walker, the woman next door and Hannah's friend, Stephen.

Thanks to Hannah, I can see. She has cut the hair round my eyes. Unfortunately, that included my eyelashes, one eye only, hence rather lop-sided looking.

19th August

Dry run in Oxford. Indy fine. I howled all night, hoping to alter Xmas plans. I didn't. Only change, Stephen no longer loves me, but will honour his promise.

Hannah believes I am too dependent on TD. Well, she's got that wrong. It's patently obvious, TD is not dependent enough on me, else she wouldn't go away and I'd never stay in Barnes or set one foot in Oxford.

Hannah says I need to wake up and get with the programme.

20th August

TD and Jacob came to collect me. It was the perfect summer's day for a riverside walk; Hannah on the mobile, TD and Jacob scouring the beach for treasure, Indy and I swimming – completely safe at low tide. Brilliant, until

Hannah decided to take us dogs home and the day turned on its head.

How could I bear the separation? I slipped my collar and dashed across the main road faster than Usain Bolt in the hundred metres. Cars from all directions came screeching to a halt as I raced to join Jacob and TD on the banks of the Thames. Hannah flew after me, leaving Indy in the hands of a stunned stranger.

We were all traumatised: the car drivers, I, Hannah, the man in charge of the abandoned dog and Indy, who believed he'd lost me forever. When eventually reunited, we lay squeezed together in a basket for one, arms entwined, hanging on to each other for dear life.

Hannah has posted our picture on Facebook. The caption: is my dog gay?

I mean. I ask you, Hannah, we're dogs.

Indy still hates the lodger but, thanks to me, likes his dog walker. Hannah has given the lodger six weeks' notice. That's the power of dogs for you. On reflection, that's the power of Indy. I must remember to thank *Barnes Running Club* for Hannah's speed.

TD has evened me up. I am now eyelashless.

TD and Hannah are panicking. We are both so accident-prone. What will happen if one of us goes? They believe whoever is left will be devastated. They needn't worry, for when that day comes, whether through age or youthful stupidity, we have it sorted. Should Indy go first, I'll have a picture of his face tattooed on my left thigh. And if I do, the more likely, being older, I shall bequeath him my favourite ball, as keepsake.

Then when both us dogs have had our day, we'll return, Indy as a stand-up comic and me his driver. Wearing a smart uniform and using my satnav skills, I shall ferry him from gig to gig, together again, together forever. Meanwhile, and always remembering the power of two, we're planning hours of fun.

21st August

Home, so distraught by the recent ordeal, am suffering incontinence. Uncle John thinks I have a urine infection. TD believes I am diabetic. I also have a sore on my lip – heading to vet for a diagnosis. Alan's away, so we're seeing the locum.

We have returned with a sample bottle. TD has to follow me round trying to catch 100ml of urine before it hits the bushes. Good luck to her. Will our friends in the park think her perverted? My sore turns out to be a wart. Over this wart we have a choice. If it's frozen off, I'll require knock-out drops costing £300, or she can tie a thread of cotton round it and attach it to a door knob and pull. I can read her mind and feel the pain.

24rd August

TD's next Am Dram production is going to be a French Farce. Farce is a posh name for comedy. It's not stand-up. Michael McIntyre won't be appearing and no one is dropping their trousers. But as it happens, a pooch is required and I'm being considered for the role, seeing the director this afternoon.

I met Pam for tea. Drank Lapsang Souchong (yuk) out of a saucer on a low table and consumed quantities of sugar. At least double my weekly ration.

Pam either owns a horse or is a keen darts player. She kept throwing lumps of sugar across the room, aiming them straight for my mouth. Bullseye! Expertly and elegantly, I caught every one. Hours of jelly-baby practice with Jacob helped.

Slight waterworks improvement: incontinence pads are heading for the bin.

25th August

I can breathe a sigh of relief. Uncle John is out of hospital. I have visited. We were both ecstatically pleased to see each other. I did not jump up. OK, I was on a choke chain.

He is now having home care. This means he is stalked

along the street by a carer who follows him at a distance of fifteen metres, checking he crosses roads safely and doesn't fall over his stick or shopping trolley. I hope this isn't some way of getting rid of the elderly, because if he forgets his green cross code, the carer will be too far away to prevent an accident.

Feeling downcast. I do now realise I should, like my brother, Branston, have trained as a mobility dog. TD says enthusiasm is no substitute for brains.

26th August

I've got it; landed the part! Was it my knowledge of French, my huge brown eyes or because I'm perfect? Oh, to be perfect, even the once.

No! It was my table manners that clinched it. I was being auditioned; the tea and sugar lumps all part of the performance – no wonder TD didn't fuss over my sugar intake. My role should have been larger, but the scene involving me rushing on and flooring the seducing villain of the piece has been cut. TD said I shouldn't be encouraged to jump up at people and if I were given a round of applause for my most ingrained habit, she'd never knock it out of me. She has a point.

There is one proviso: my hair. I can't look like a fleabag. I'm taking the part of a *Kennel Club* poodle called Fifi. I'm playing a girl, for heaven's sake, prostituting myself for my art. TD is finding out where Shirty Bertie goes. This time I'll need a proper poodle cut.

Mustn't screw up. If I do they'll hand my part to a greyhound and stick a rug on it.

27th August

We were off to Poodelicious; a spring in my step, TD in combative mood. It wasn't a promising exchange.

'I've never seen anything so disgusting in all my life.' Oh, come on, wasn't I there to be washed? Actually, the woman looked quite poodle-like herself; top knot and fluffy slippers. Almost checked round her back to see if she had a tail.

'He's been deflead.'

The woman shuddered. It was time for a gear change. TD offered her a ticket for the opening night and a free advert in the programme. I put on my most seductive smile: head cocked, mouth open, tongue protruding slightly – always a winner. We work so well as a team.

'I'm not risking my reputation on a dog like that.' Our attempts to ingratiate ourselves were going nowhere but we kept calm and carried on. I hung my head in anticipation as TD inhaled deeply and exhaled plan B; if in doubt cheat, or in this case, lie. That owner of mine is so predictable.

'He's a rescue dog, found roaming the streets, starved and unloved.' Seriously! I thanked God dogs don't blush. 'If only you could work your magic, he could star in the Blackheath show.' Oh please, I'm on at the end of Act 2. This was more humiliating than I'd feared.

The woman saw right through her argument and the door closed firmly behind us. Our campaign was foundering. It was back to the drawing-board. Fortunately for me, TD is no quitter. Hannah says she's like a dog with a bone. There are times I'm proud to be owned by her.

28ᵗʰ August

I've lost my looks! My mouth is so full of warts it looks like an ancient cave filled with stalactites. It could have been a crowd-puller in days of old, when fairgrounds showed dogs with three heads and monkeys growing out of armpits – did Jacob really get his facts straight? It was back in the olden days, before he was born. Anyway, we're off to the vet with cash, credit card and cheque book.

Alan's advice was, vile though they look, to leave them. In a couple of days the mouth will say, 'Hi, warts!' and proceed to produce its own antibiotic, then bingo, they'll disappear. We dogs are miracle creatures. TD sold him a wad of tickets for my show.

29th August

Park gossip is getting right up my snout. Just don't get me involved in the race debate – all this Romanian-Bulgarian argy-bargy nonsense. When it comes to immigration, I'm totally impartial. Well, so I should be: Miriam's from Bratislava, Sharon's from Glasgow and Ivana, Croatia. There are a few Spanish rescue dogs in the park, nervous, otherwise well-behaved. So, no problems there, but what if these millions of Bulgarians and Romanians bring their dogs? If their owners arrive, hopeful for work, are unable to find a job and receive no benefit for three months, will their dogs be thrown on to the streets?

There should be a large notice at Passport Control and all places of embarkation saying, BATTERSEA IS FULL.

And another point: will these dogs carry diseases, be rabid or have Alabama rot, the new virus found in woods? Dead in a week! No medication available. Their countries have more trees than people.

30th August

Alan was right. My mouth is wart-free; I could smile for a toothpaste ad. Bring on the cameras, let the paparazzi loose!

If I wasn't busy enough with this acting life, TD has a big cooking job on, so it's off to Barnes for me. I knew something was up the moment I clapped eyes on my little friend, shivering in his basket. Jacks was ill, noisily ill. I could picture the scene deteriorating fast, past experience and all that.

Well, we were soundly asleep in our separate beds, Hannah in her room, me and Indy in the kitchen, when the calls began. Yep, my hunch was proving right.

'Hans, my throat, get me an ice-lolly from the freezer. Hans, I'm dying.' I can identify with that.

Hannah was in and out of bed, running this way and that. Indy, up and down like a jack-in-the-box, following Hannah from room to room. I dozed. Someone had to keep their cool.

31ˢᵗ August. 7 a.m.

Woken by loud banging and toilet flushing, then Jacks drove to A&E with overnight bag, confident they would keep her in. I wasn't holding my breath. Indy crossed his trembling paws.

Hannah took one look at her hysterical hound and made a snap decision. Anything, even yoga, was worth a try. Does her teacher seriously consider meditation calming for pets?

We sat in a circle, Hannah in the lotus position, unachievable for dogs, even the supple Indy. Then Hannah began to hum, 'Ommmm…' and, well, I couldn't believe my ears. Indy joined in 'Ommmmmm…' Trust him to catch on to Velantra Mantra. Had he done this before or was he a real smart arse? Nooo! He was as clueless as me. He wasn't chanting at all, merely sound asleep, snoring his head off.

Filled with a new positive energy, we headed to the common for a quick walk, returning via the shops. Out of lollies, no stopping, Hannah was voting with her feet. Personally, I prefer ice-cream; Magnum Classic.

Peace short-lived. About to get our heads down when the front door flew open and Jacks was back with antibiotics, furious at the NHS for keeping her waiting seven whole hours. Hannah told her she was lucky not to live in Wales, where waiting times are longer.

8 p.m.

Another frightful night was well under way as Jacks felt the need to share her pain; coughing, crying, moaning, bedroom door wide open. Indy so upset we were allowed to sleep on Hannah's bed.

1ˢᵗ September. 8 a.m.

The nose blowing began. I have never seen so much toilet paper in all my life – no truly, even on Andrex ads. Jacks worked faster than a factory worker on a production line, wrapping the paper round her hand like a bandage, one blow, then tossed it on the floor. The only let-up was when she stopped for pills or Pepsi.

Six hours later a pile of paper balls filled the entire spare room. Jacks invisible, lost somewhere in the pyramid of snot-filled tissue, only the constant trumpeting proof she was still alive.

2.30 p.m.
Off for a run in Richmond Park. If Indy chases the deer he will be shot. This would add to the agony of the day.

4 p.m.
Left park. The deer OK. Indy OK. Home to an empty flat. 'Hallelujah!' cried Hannah, the word barely died on her lips before Jacks, still in her PJs, struggled in with *Sainsbury's* bags.

7 p.m.
Jacks took over the kitchen, cooking and eating her way through pizzas, pot noodles, grated cheese, garlic bread and trifle. The entire stock of *Sainsbury's Local* going down her gullet. We watched, first in awe, then in horror as all the food came back up. Vomit. Sick as a dog, head in a bag. She was back to A& E by ambulance.

Jacks' exit from Hannah's flat was speedier than even Indy had hoped.

2ⁿᵈ September
I have to take my hat off to the little fellow; he's a bigger man than me.

After the Jacks debacle, Hannah needed to let her hair down. Fair dos, except it was a work night and involved vodka shots. No surprise therefore that Hannah, after excessive alcohol consumption at the *Tart Bar*, arrived home late. It wasn't a sleep-in-your-clothes-night, so that was something, but she failed us on the breakfast front.

By the time Indy took charge of the situation, Hannah was late for work, in the bath, trying to feel half human. Can warm water do that? Anyway, Indy took my bowl – yes, my bowl – carried it into the bathroom and shoved it under her nose. And it worked: we were fed. For this I give him my heartfelt thanks. I believe he is more altruistic than me.

Tomorrow, I'm back to the moderate calm of Greenwich life, with its promise of haircuts, rehearsals and instant fame. Can't wait!

6ᵗʰ September

Where's Annette's gung-ho spirit? She's been bending TD's ear for hours.

The old girl awoke panic-stricken. Overcome by age, too close to death to own a pet, she visited *Lady Tabitha's Kitty Emporium*; the stroke-a-cat-over-a-cup-of-tea café in Dulwich. They're looking for seven cats, why not Kiki? Unfortunately for Annette, the cat showed its true colours and bit the owners, Sarah and Sandra.

At that point, Annette was severely admonished, told in no uncertain terms they were looking for strays, preferably those with a missing paw or one eye, real sad tales. They weren't there for elderly ladies to offload their crabby cats.

Annette fled, tail between legs, carrying the said pet, who, having crapped the whole way there, succeeded, without any additional food, to crap the whole way back. Are the words Kiki and pet synonymous? If Annette doesn't get off the blower soon, I'll never be fed. Have tried every trick in the book to grab her attention; jumping up, scratching, even attempted bringing up bile, but the talk continues.

If rats, cockroaches and cats are to inherit the earth, does this include Kiki?

7ᵗʰ September

Skates are usually considered a speedy mode of transport, except in Jacob's case. He spent most of his time flat on his back or hugging trees. I had no walk to speak of, but thought it best to stay shtum.

Leaving me and the skates at home, they shot off to town, to museums where dogs aren't permitted. I didn't want to go, anyway. The *Natural History Museum* being the exception; you can get in if you are stuffed. In which case, I really didn't want to go. When they returned clutching balloons and smelling of Quarter Pounders and Happy Meals, I wished I had. I hate to miss a party.

8ᵗʰ September

What's going on? I may be the most patient, placid, long-suffering dog in the whole of the northern hemisphere, but this takes the biscuit. TD's only buggered off to Paris with the family and left me with my minder.

'Jack shall have Jill. Naught shall go ill. The dog shall have TD again. And all shall be well.'

10ᵗʰ September

Will this madness ever leave her? The family only treats her to a weekend break in Disney, allows her out, loose in Paris, for a day's sightseeing. She alights at Les Halles/Chatelet, the perfect location for the Louvre, Pompidou Centre, Notre Dame and Tuileries gardens. She turns her back on the lot, walks into a pet shop and buys a dog.

The rest of the day is spent finding all the ways she can't get the puppy back. Am I living with a child?

11ᵗʰ September

TD is home. I am home. The puppy marooned in Paris. OK, in a shop. TD believed she could take it on Eurostar, assumed its passport was in order. Instead, she and Hannah will collect it by ferry once the show is over. The family's tearing their hair out. She's really done it this time; there's no way they'd dream of taking her on holiday again.

Heard it all! When TD stood up before the family court, her plea was this: Uncle John had given her fifty quid as a thank you. Told her, 'Go buy yourself some flowers, anything you want.' No mention of four legs, I might add. Later, when cross-examined further, she cited me in her defence. I'd not been myself since Indy left and needed a friend. It was the right dog, at the right time, in the wrong place.

My few grey cells were busy working overtime, attempting to absorb this startling piece of information. Not been myself, lonely, a puppy – a lost little girl needing love and attention? Ooh la-la! French-speaking, of course!

So TD knew what was wrong, all along. I'm a pack animal and needed a mate. All those months spent putting up a brave front. I felt my four legs push me off the ground and up I went. A descendent of the circus poodles, Cookie and Ruiliz; soaring up above the lions and clowns, over the trapeze, the high wires, out of the big top and into the sky. And when at last my feet touched solid ground, my mind continued to float high above the clouds.

My bounce was back. Watch out park, here I come. And Indy, you needn't worry: whatever happens, you'll always be my best mate.

12ᵗʰ September

I must be perfect; it's seven and a half months since my last sock episode. Jacob's last tantrum, a mere two and a half months ago, confirming my behaviour is improving at a faster rate than his. Mercifully for mankind, Jacob's training continues. TD has stopped all mine.

Annette is so appalled by her own conduct she has taken to her bed. TD is doing food runs for pet and owner. Will she be out of bed before Kiki's party in October? Am I invited, or is it a cat only occasion? TD must rue the day she ever learnt to cook.

As our search for a cheap and cheerful haircut goes on, my admiration for her continues to rise.

13ᵗʰ September

'*I must to the barber's, monsieur; for methinks I am marvellous hairy...*' Shakespeare could have written these lines for me.

After our *Poodelicious* slap in the face, I left the house clean as a whistle, covered in products, not produce. We marched past *Scruffs 2 Crufts* and zoomed straight into the

Bridge Lane Barbers, where TD, who'd spent weeks honing her powers of persuasion, threw an offer on the table. A double-page ad in the programme would up their game. They'd undercut the pricey *Blackheath* hairdressers and steal their trade. No one loves a bargain better than the rich. Add on free parking and bingo.

Would they seize the opportunity, smell the scent of success and cut my hair?

The young South London Cypriot boys and the North Kent girls, old enough to be their grans, had sod-all in common till we walked in – Greeks bearing gifts. The vote was a resounding yes. I'd be their first joint venture, receive a complete makeover, nothing too extreme. I'm not entering a creative competition.

Who had the larger team now, Boris with his Eastern Europeans, or me, in the experienced hands of Sheila and Shirley, Josef, Hasan and Mustafa, the golden girls of Kent, the Adonises of Lewisham?

I stood on a table in front of the long mirror, watching the clippers zip through my matted coat. Thank goodness my eyelashes had grown back. Spellbound, I monitored my transformation: pom-pommed feet and tail, topknot with bow and, finally, a sculpted butt. Then over to the ladies for a wash and blow-dry under a massive mushroom, tea and cake, of course.

We left them, five heads bent over the table, the blonde and the black, two dyed, three not, pooling the energy of youth and experience of age as they planned their future enterprise. A salon for pets and their owners.

I have to admit to feeling a little odd, like a teenager who's outgrown his old body but is unfamiliar with the new; in my case, a transitory state, and one to enjoy while I can, for the moment the show is over, out will come the scissors and off will go the fluff. I'm already booked in for a dental check.

I hope I don't catch a chill from my hairless bottom. Actors don't miss rehearsals and the show opens next month. The whole family will be there for my fifteen minutes of fame. Mrs King swears she wouldn't miss it for the world and is flying back from Spain, especially. Not Indy. Hannah says he'd prefer to stay home and watch a programme on canine prisoners of war.

14th September

Whoops, behind with all non-theatre diary entries. How very remiss. Has acting gone to my head, the world of the theatre taken over from real life?

Latest info: Annette's been unable to give any of her friends a lift for two whole weeks. The stench of Kiki crap lives on.

More exciting is, now we are three, Oxford can't take us. So Indy, the new puppy and I will be spending Christmas on a Welsh beach with his dog minder. I shall return smelling of salt and sand, which TD says will make a pleasant change. Will our new girl be carsick? Wales is on the other side of the country. If my back has to act as an anti-sickness pill, she'll need a ladder to reach it. If it's a five-hour drive, could we please do it lying down?

15th September

We're living in the dark, no television, only the radio for entertainment – not a money-saving strategy, for once. TD has an inflamed eyes; bright red, stuck solid. I'm convinced a bit of saliva would help, but she refuses to let me lick them. The world, including Uncle John, has told her to go to A&E – advice she has ignored. If she loses her sight, she will receive no sympathy. If she goes totally blind, I shall have to retrain as a guide dog.

Can an old dog learn new tricks?

16th September

Today I made a decision, a grown-up one. I'm going to stop all my hypochondria. I've written it down in black and white. It's there for posterity. All I have to do is stick to it. I'm panicking already.

17th September

Was I right or was I right? I am definitely psychic. This French girl is a rescue dog, originally from Eastern Europe – Bucharest no less – dumped in Paris.

If France is already experiencing this dog invasion, Britain better watch out. We're OK, we've picked the cream, or should I say, crème de la crème; a healthy, rabies-free bitch, but what about the thousands of others? I knew the subject hadn't been given a proper airing.

I'm informed this puppy looks like a hairy rat. Not one rat, but two joined together like bendy buses. Sounds implausible; does it have six legs? English will be the puppy's third language – has it more brain cells than me? Insecurity has hit a new low.

18th September

Deeply relieved. TD has recovered; she requires neither white stick nor guide dog.

19th September

It's a wrap: first rehearsal over, walking on air.

Shared a dressing room with Katie, the actress who escorts me on stage – already a huge fan. We hung about in the Green Room, a space smaller than our garden, that isn't green. Most of the actors wandered about, noses in books, muttering, far too busy to say hello to a dog, even if said dog was a fellow thespian. Katie says they'll chat more once they've learnt their lines.

My part demands sitting very still and listening to a long conversation, then on my cue, 'Let's adjourn!' I rise, walk over to a low table and drink daintily from an antique tea cup. This was the tricky bit, where being a dog let me down. I used my tongue as a Brillo pad on a dirty saucepan. Once I'd realised I wouldn't be thrown any sugar lumps until I'd stopped sucking the life out of it, I got it. Three sugar lumps later, I lie down beside a sofa called a chaise longue (new addition to French vocab). And there I remain, without falling asleep, till the curtain falls. Now I've conquered the teacup routine, as a creature of habit I shouldn't need many rehearsals.

Then off we all went to the *Railway Tavern*, one mad dash to get a drink in before closing time. Naturally, I refused beer but accepted crisps – beef, I believe.

Bus home, rushed up to the top deck to reserve the front seats. You get the best views from there.

'What a handsome dog,' said a woman seated beside TD.

'Oh! He doesn't normally look like that.' While TD explained, I sat, nose against window, ignoring the traffic for once. My body was on the bus, my mind back in the theatre, treading the boards. With a mention in the *Evening Standard*, or dare I hope a glowing review, would I bag an agent? OMG, was I star-struck! Had I caught the acting bug? There's talk of a tour in the spring.

'Good grief!' exclaimed the woman, her voice on the loudspeaker button. 'A dog in a play! Are you mad or extremely brave?' The entire bus turned to listen.

'Excuse me.' I could see TD's temper rising. I bit my tongue.

'Have you forgotten the words of Gracie Fields?' The woman paused dramatically; the passengers waited with baited breath. 'Never work with animals or children.'

Why didn't TD bite her? I wanted to. Stupid woman, what does she know about life?

20th September

Now I've caught the conjunctivitis bug and am stretched out on the sofa, suffering. It's real, not hypochondria. Truly, I'm highly contagious. Optrex is being administered hourly, otherwise different rules apply. We're living in the light with the TV on. Photophobia doesn't count when it comes to me. How will I cope under stage lighting? I have the patience of a saint.

Turns out I'm going to need it. This French puppy has spent nine months in different cages in Europe. Is not house-trained. Has never seen a blade of grass, chased a squirrel, worn a collar or caught a ball. I can see I'm going to have my paws full.

21st September

Next week is the Dress, a rehearsal I don't need to dress for, except for the collar, diamanté, blue not pink. My name has changed from Fifi to Fido. I'm not exactly hung like a donkey – in truth, I'm not really hung at all. But my remaining piece of tackle was a bit of a giveaway. Can't say the name change has altered my performance.

When we run through the curtain call, TD has insisted I'm on the lead. If the applause intoxicates my brain, she fears I'll jump off the stage and rush about, greeting the audience.

23rd September

The infection has gone, my sight returned to 20:20 vision. I feared if it continued, I might have needed an understudy. Not that greyhound dressed in a rug! No way; let it stick to running. Besides, I'm a real trouper; I'd have performed on my deathbed and worn dark glasses.

24th September

TD read it in *The Stage*, so it has to be gospel. *Downton Abbey* is looking for a pooch for their next series. She's not known as a pushy parent, but on this occasion? Please, please, paws crossed. Their casting director is coming to see our show. Might it launch a stellar career? If the bus lady got to see me on TV, that'd sure make her sit up and beg.

The show opens Monday. Once the final curtain comes down, we're off to collect our puppy from Paris then drive on to Brittany, which, I've checked, is in France. It's going to be one epic journey and a major challenge. Not knowing my way past Cité Europe, my satnav skills will be of zero help.

26th September

As the play opens in four days' time, I'm doing my best to keep focused. TD is not. All her energies are directed elsewhere: France. The shopping has echoes of Christmas. The spare room is jammed with puppy stuff; toys, chews, posh bedding. Was I ever this spoilt? It's not a question of jealousy. No, absolutely not. OK, all this 'rescue puppy' talk is beyond crazy, but it'll pass. No, what really gets me down, sick to the stomach, right where my goolies were – is the offer of crates. Not one, but hundreds.

'Still in its wrapping.' 'We never use it.' 'Only slightly broken.' 'Oh go on, please have it.' OK, so people are generous. But does that mean we have to accept them all? And if we do, where will we store them?

I dwelt on the subject, my brain in overdrive, the seconds ticking away. Before a minute was up, I'd solved the problem. We'd create an erection like Amish Kapoor and open our garden to the public. Couldn't be hard to build; his Olympic park sculpture is only bits of twisted steel.

Whoa there, Dougal, stop! Pea-brained – I don't think so. Alan has to have it wrong. I must have more brain cells than even TD.

27ᵗʰ September

I'm driven to the park most mornings, rather like a celebrity off to his gala screening in a stretch limo. Except, no one would call our nose-smeared, muddy car (my fault) with scratched hubcaps (her fault), state of the art. But I enjoy it. Find the traffic and people-watching beneficial for the soul. Possibly not as good as pavement-walking for filing the nails, but who cares about toenails, certainly not me. And, whether sun, rain, wind or snow, the one constant is the radio. And that today was what mattered, the subject fungi. According to the radio, foraging for fungi is devastating the countryside. Oh really! Not as I see it.

Do we have fungi in Greenwich Park? Yes. Do people pick them? No. Do dogs eat them? No. I wanted to phone in, give them my POV and put them straight.

In Greenwich, the locals unable to differentiate between fungi the size of dinner plates and the delicate mauve ones sensibly desist from picking. And we dogs, who are less informed on their dangers, are prevented from having any impact on the local ecology or making deadly choices by the toadstool's utter lack of scent. Hence our surprise at being chased up One Tree Hill by an American tourist, dying to know if I was an Italian truffle-hunting dog.

'I wish,' said TD. It sounded important and exceedingly tasty, so I wished too. But are there any truffles in Greenwich Park? Or did the American lady think she was in Tuscany?

28th September

Despite fears she may need extra oxygen, Mrs King has bravely booked her flight from Malaga. She has given TD her word she'll be armed with plenty of asthma medication.

We don't want her dying during the show.

29th September

Tech and dress. It's been one long day.

Mustn't get drawn into the hype of this glitzy showbiz world; need to keep my sights on simpler things, the realities of life such as…well, food and er…what else? My brain's shut down. I believe Labs think about food every six seconds, so being half a Lab, let's call it twelve. That's a shedload of food thoughts during the waking day. I bet the quality improves with a second dog and what about treats? Herta Frankfurter Sausages are simply the best. Oh, I'm so into my brands.

Need to get over my crate phobia, pronto. News is: I'm to sleep in one with the puppy until it becomes adjusted. Well, if this puppy needs me, so be it. That is my duty. If nothing else it will keep me grounded. I'm feeling more sensible already.

Mrs King called from Malaga airport to say she may not make it. She arrived early, had a quick one to steady her nerves. 'Ginebra, por favor.' Three words of Spanish she'd picked up during her months away. Tanked up and legless – oh, I remember that feeling – she'd tottered through departures, placed her hand-luggage in a tray and waited to be frisked. Alarms went off. The scanner viewing her belongings stopped in its tracks. Five security officers dived into a bag packed with inhalers – reliever and preventative – and box upon box of theophylline tablets. Assuming the old lady to be a mule working for a well-known drug runner, she was taken away for questioning.

Mrs King, who was having no truck with Spanish officials, told them straight: it was imperative she board the next flight. And if they dared to stop her, the entire Conservative Party would hold them personally responsible. She would not miss seeing her Dougal starring in a West End play for all the tea in China.

'D…D…Donovan ? Jason Donovan?'

'Dougal. Not that Ozzie singing eejit. Dougal.' Mrs King had no time for Spanish stupidity.

'Jason Donovan?'

'Are you deaf, young man? Dougal. My friend, Dougal. The dog called Dougal.' Mrs King was allowed to call a solicitor, but chose instead to phone me, wanting to inform me she might not make it. It was then they dropped the charges, deciding they were best rid of her. Spain had enough of its own problems without the British dumping their nutcases on them.

Hooray, Ma King is on her way.

30th September

As the curtain rose on Act 2 and sounds of applause and laughter poured through the tannoy, Katie and I remained in our dressing room waiting for our call. Katie, clothed in a gypsy-style wedding dress much like the one Titch wore to Bertie's birthday, was studying the script, again. Not me. I put the time to better use. Velantra Mantra? Not really my thing, more like, a chance '*to sleep, perchance to dream*', or doze, dream and quietly hum, "Dum, dum, dum, de dum, de…" Cliff Richard's *Summer Holiday* song was buzzing round my head and might have gone on ad infinitum, but luckily for Katie, the tannoy interrupted my drone.

'Miss Johnson and Mr Dougal to the stage, please.'

'Wake up, Dougal, we're on!' I leapt to attention. Katie took me by the lead and the handsome pair walked along the corridor, up a flight of stairs and on to the stage, two heads held proud, one tail wagging, to join the buzz, excitement, applause and laughter.

As I looked out into the auditorium, I was amazed to see a crowd double the size of Wimbledon's Centre Court. And in the front row, Jacob and Uncle John waving, Aunt Annette wolf-whistling and old Ma King, puffer in hand, shouting, coughing and wheezing. The old girl had made it! I almost broke loose and joined them, but sense prevailed – my show-off moment was coming up any second now.

Cool as a cucumber and breathing deeply, I supped tea as delicately as any a dog is able to. Then I positioned myself, mouth open, tongue hanging attractively down, primed for the first sugar lump to fly my way. You could have heard a pin drop.

And up I leapt, soaring high into the rafters as only a part-poodle can. Cameras flashed, applause thundered, Jacob stood on his seat, then Uncle John and the two old girls, followed by the entire audience, rose to their feet yelling, 'Encore, Dougal, encore, encore.' What had Murray and Djokovic got on me? It was an ovation, a standing ovation, my ovation. If only my French puppy had been there to watch.

THE END

Dougal's Acknowledgements

First, my enormous thanks to Crooked Cat Publishing. For a cat company to be interested in a story written by a dog is truly amazing. Since they were able to swallow their prejudices and publish my book, I've had to square it with my conscience and seriously review my attitude to cats. This has been tricky, but I've managed it. I do, however, have qualms over the 'crooked' word. Are they urgently in need of a vet or heading to a young offenders' institution? These concerns I'm trying to keep at the back of my mind.

To my mate, Jacob, for nicking me biscuits from *Pets at Home* and for the hours of fun we've spent being bad boys together.

My thanks to the Greenwich Players for having me in their Christmas show. Not as the back end of a donkey, but a dog named Scruff. It's the story of an orphan and his dog, searching for shelter and love. A 'no room at the inn' tale: sad with a happy ending. The part requires me to look as dirty, disgusting and smelly as possible. Right up my street. Mud, mud, here I come!

Thanks, too, to Hannah, Uncle John, Indy, Princess Miriam, my dog walker, and Alan, my vet. Plus all my other friends: the lovely Lois, Maggie, Annette, Mrs King and all the kind people who throw balls for me every day in Greenwich Park.

To The Write Place, for letting me attend their classes for an entire month, right up to the night I foolishly blew it. I cocked my leg against the tea urn and wasn't allowed back, despite the vote of confidence going my way. Thank you, Elaine Everest, you taught me a lot.

Apologies

To the baby whose ice-cream I stole. Sorry, but you were too young to be eating one. And a good lesson to learn at an early age: life is unfair. The sooner you accept that, the better. Well, that's what I've been told. By the way, it was delicious.

Fantastic Books
Great Authors

CROOKED
CAT

Meet our authors and discover
our exciting range:

- Gripping Thrillers
- Cosy Mysteries
- Romantic Chick-Lit
- Fascinating Historicals
- Exciting Fantasy
- Young Adult and Children's
  Adventures

8540070R00081

Printed in Germany
by Amazon Distribution
GmbH, Leipzig